T0198924

SHIPWRECKED & STRANDED

ROBERT LAILHEUGUE

WESTBOW
PRESS®
A DIVISION OF THOMAS NELSON
& ZONDERVAN

WestBow Press books may be ordered through booksellers or by contacting:

WestBow Press
A Division of Thomas Nelson & Zondervan
1663 Liberty Drive
Bloomington, IN 47403
www.westbowpress.com
1 (866) 928-1240

Interior Image Credit: Richard Lane

ISBN: 978-1-9736-8340-7 (sc)
ISBN: 978-1-9736-8341-4 (hc)
ISBN: 978-1-9736-8339-1 (e)

Library of Congress Control Number: 2020900460

Print information available on the last page.

WestBow Press rev. date: 01/20/2020

DEDICATIONS

This book is dedicated to the men and women who have met God, received His grace but threw it all aside to chase after careers and their own desires. They may have left God, but He has not abandoned them. Listen to His calling; whatever you have done, He is willing to forgive. He just asks that we repent and return to His open arms.

ACKNOWLEDGMENTS

I must, above all things, give thanks and glory to my Lord and Savior Jesus Christ, who has presented me with the opportunity to write this Christian based novel. It is He, who keeps me focused and dedicated to presenting a story that is both entertaining and brings a positive message into a troubled world.

I would, also, like to thank my wonderful illustrator, Richard Lane, who provided all the artwork for this book. I look forward to working with him on future projects. If interested in his work, perhaps for one of your own projects, he can be reached by e-mail at lane2212@bellsouth.net or on Facebook under his name.

And I thank God for my friend and proofreader, Ken Peters, who did the spell check on this book.

And I must give a special thank you to Debbie Lane, who was the editor for this project; she spent many hours working on the manuscript, providing excellent input and guidance. Debbie did an outstanding job.

Ken, Debbie, Richard and I all go the same church- The Harbor Church, Hammond, LA. Thanks again to those wonderful Christian brothers and sisters.

Last, but not least, I must thank my lovely wife of fifty years Debra Lailheugue. We have raised a family, and have gone through both good times and bad times together. Now, she gives me space to write and study God's Word. She serves as a sounding board during the writing process and is the self proclaimed "number one fan" of my books. Love you Debbie!

FOREWORD

Have you ever wondered how you would react, or what you would do if you found yourself all alone on an uninhabited tropical island? We are about to find out how one man handled that very situation; and the extraordinary means that he would employ to survive. Help would come in the most unusual forms. But, in the end, he learned that deliverance would have to come from within.

CHAPTER ONE

THE BEACH

We find Stan lying face down on a small deserted island. He lay there on the sandy beach where he had been washed up on the shore barely hanging onto life. He was wearing the latest pair of Nike deck shoes, a nice pair of designer shorts, and a designer shirt to match; he wore the newest model Rolex watch and a big diamond cluster ring. He looked cool; he looked like a man of success. At least he did a few days earlier, when he was standing at the helm aboard his big, thirty five foot sport fishing boat equipped twin inboard-outboard engines and a flying bridge with top-of-the line navigation equipment. Below deck was a full galley, a head with shower, and bunk room that could sleep four people. He had all the latest fishing gear onboard and was ready for a good time. He was headed for the Bahamas on an extended fishing vacation with three of his best and closest friends.

As Stan was lying face down in the sand, his wallet was still in his pants pocket. He had several credit cards and $400 in cash; he could buy anything, but there was nothing to buy here on this empty beach. He had his driver's license and the keys to his fast, new, red Chevy Corvette parked back in Florida; but there were not any cars here either. Of course, he had the latest model I-phone, but it was full of sea water and even if it did work, which it didn't, there was no service out here in the middle of this ocean. In addition to these now useless things, Stan was wearing an orange life vest that apparently saved him from drowning, or so he thought. The life vest contained a basic survival kit in the pocket that included a small pack of matches, fishing line, two fishhooks, a small knife, a two hand wire saw, and a small flashlight. At least it was something.

Back in the States, Stan had a wife and two children. He had been a big boss on the job, he was paid well by the company he worked for, and he had learned how to manage his money. He owned a nice house and had all the "toys" of a successful American worker and manager. Back on the job, all he had to do was pick up the phone and direct someone else to handle any situation that arose; but, here, there is no phone, or anyone to call. Anything that needed to be done would have to be done by him. At work, when the opportunity came up, he was able to retire at a very young age. There would be plenty time to enjoy the rewards of his successful career. But now, he finds himself barely alive, lying on this deserted beach of an island in the middle of God only knows where.

Just three days earlier, Stan and three buddies were on their way to that long awaited extended fishing trip and three weeks of partying in the islands. Everyone onboard was having a good time; until that terrible, unpredicted storm quickly came upon them out of nowhere. A lightning bolt knocked out all the craft's electrical systems and the engines were "dead in the water". The boat was tossed about in fifteen foot waves like a ball in a hot potato contest. Then, suddenly, a fire broke out in the engine compartment followed by a huge explosion; which knocked everyone out of the boat and into the raging sea. Within minutes the boat sank to the bottom of the sea like a stone.

At the time of the explosion, Stan's buddies were on the forward deck trying to get the life raft free of its mooring straps. Stan remained at the helm trying to control the boat as best he could. When Stan was thrown into the water, he was knocked unconscious and did not see if his friends made it into the raft or not. He hoped they had made it into the relative safety of the raft. Once the seas had calmed down, Stan drifted for three days floating in his life vest. The storm had pushed them hundreds of miles off course; so, there wasn't much hope that a search party would even be looking for them in this area of the sea, or at all, for that matter. Nobody would even know that they would be missing for at least twenty more days when they don't return home.

Stan rolled over on his back; and while looking up at the sky he yelled out, "God why have You done this to me?"

Stan didn't know it at the time, but God had not abandoned him. In fact, God had brought him to this place to raise him up. It was not by chance, that Stan landed on this very special island, that is not even identified on any navigation chart, situated somewhere between the Atlantic Ocean and the Caribbean Sea. Stan would later find out that "his island" could sustain life, and he was not the only inhabitant on the island. There were monkeys: special monkeys that could talk, and, oh, would they talk.

But for now, Stan could only lay here and reflect on his past life- a life, a time, and loved ones, that he did not know if he would ever see again.

CHAPTER TWO

THE ASSESSMENT

It was a couple of hours that Stan laid on the beach before he even moved. He was drifting in and out of consciousness. He was exhausted from the days spent in the sea and the heat from the burning sun beating down on him; but now that he was on land, he could not seem to muster up enough energy to move off the hot sand. Once, when he awoke from his deep sleep, he saw two coconuts lying next to him which he did not remember seeing there before. Then, he remembered the pocket knife in his survival kit.

Stan retrieved the survival kit, removed the pocket knife, and used it to bore a hole into the "eye" of one coconut. The coconut milk was like sweet nectar to his parched palette; he savored the juice as he let it slowly wash over his parched tongue and down his dry throat. After finishing his coconut milk, Stan started to assess his current situation. The first order of business was to get off the hot sandy beach; if not, he would surely die from sun exposure and heat exhaustion.

The coconut milk had given Stan enough energy to very slowly move himself off the beach to the shade within the trees which were approximately thirty yards from the water's edge. There he found a nice tree that provided relief from the blistering sun. He flopped to the ground and leaned his back against the tree. After resting for a few minutes, he again took out his pocket knife and bored a hole into his second coconut. As with the first, Stan drank every drop of milk the coconut had to offer. He then broke both coconuts open on a large nearby rock exposing the pure white meat inside. Stan dined on the fresh coconut and could not ever remember having a better meal in his life. When he finished eating; he fell back to sleep.

He slept through the night and was awakened by the noonday sun well overhead and the gentle waves from the sea lapping at the shore nearby.

Stan looking down a stretch
of empty beach.

Stan thought to himself, "Under any other circumstances this would be a beautiful, tranquil beach. But, for now, I have to build up my strength, go find a town, and figure out where I am; so, I can call for some help. The first order of business will be to call my family to let them know what happened; and that I'm alright. If they know I'm missing, they will be worried sick. And maybe they will have some news about my fishing buddies. I sure hope they are all safe. But first things first; I need to get strong enough to walk out of here. No telling how far the nearest people are."

Stan didn't see any more coconuts lying on the beach, but there were plenty coconut trees around. Stan went in search of coconuts, which he thought would be easy to locate based on his good fortune of finding those lying next to him on the sand. He saw numerous fruit high up in the trees; however, very few were on the ground.

He thought, "The wind must have blown those coconuts to where I had been washed up on the beach. After all I have been through; it's about time I get a little 'lucky'. But, for now, I have to eat enough food so that I can travel. I don't know if I landed on an island; or if I'm in some country in South or Central American, or perhaps Mexico. Wherever I am, I hope the people speak at least a little English; so, I will be able to communicate with them."

There was no way Stan could climb the trees to obtain the coconuts that were high up in the foliage. He would have to rely on what he could find on the ground.

As Stan gathered the few coconuts he could find, he thought; "What an excellent food source for traveling. The coconut comes neatly packaged in its own nature-made container, both meat and beverage in one durable wrapping. You can't beat this.

But, there was one little problem in the back of his mind that was starting to eat away at him; over the three days that he had been here on the beach, he had not seen one boat pass by on the water or even a plane flying overhead. There weren't any signs of civilization in the area that he had seen thus far. And there was one other thing, Stan had a strong feeling that someone or something was watching him from within the heavy cover of the vegetation. He would look, but never see anything; he had this eerie feeling that there was always "eyes on him".

Good thing Stan had been a Boy Scout; he had learned some basic skills about survival that will come in handy. While he was gathering coconuts, he also harvested some small vines that he could use to make a container to carry his precious cargo of coconuts. He used the vines to weave an enclosure for the bottom of his life vest; that way he could place the coconuts inside his new container and sling the vest over his shoulder with one of the vest straps. He was pleased with his invention.

CHAPTER THREE

SEARCH FOR HELP

With a "backpack" full of coconuts, it was time to make a decision on which direction to travel. Picking the right way could bring him into a populated area where he could find help; however, traveling in the wrong direction could lead him deeper into unoccupied territory. Basically, he had three travel options: follow the coastline north or south, or go inland to the mountains. He figured that his best chance of finding civilization was going to be somewhere along the coast, but where? After carefully weighing the options available to him, he decided to take the inland route to the mountain top.

Stan chose the mountains for one main reason. The mountain top would give him a high observation position to better survey the area and possibly pinpoint the site of a village or town. He estimated the mountain range to be about 400 feet at its highest point; at least it looked that way from where he stood on the beach. So, with his "backpack" slung over his shoulder, Stan struck out for the mountains. He didn't have to go far into the trees, before he could feel the ground starting to rise under his feet as it reached up to meet the mountain range.

Within forty five minutes of leaving the beach, Stan was standing on a barren rock at the mountaintop. Stan was now aware of one of his biggest unspoken fears; he was stranded on an island. It was a small island at that. He estimated the island to be about fifteen miles long and maybe three quarters of a mile at its widest point. The small mountain range ran for about eight miles down the center of the island and was surrounded by thick jungle on both sides and at both ends. And to make matters worse, Stand did not see any signs of life from where he was standing. And he could not see any other islands in every direction he looked.

Being the optimist that Stan is, he refused to give up. He thought that even if this is an uninhabited island, it may be visited by fisherman from some other unseen islands in area. If so, they would most likely have set up a camp somewhere along the beach.

Stan thought, "And if there is a camp, I'll have to walk around the whole island until I find it." Joking with himself Stan said, "I'll have to check my events calendar to see when I can schedule a walk around the island." Laughing he said, "Oh my calendar is clear; I should be able to start sometime soon, like perhaps right now."

Before he left the mountaintop, Stan looked over the vastness of the sea in all directions and he said, "Somewhere out there is my family, and somehow I will get back to them." He thought, "It's funny how we take for granted those we love most, when we are among them. Sometimes, it takes a separation with the real possibility that we may never see them, again, for us to realize their true value to us and just how much we truely love them. I wish I had loved harder, told them I appreciated them more, and showed more affection towards my family. God willing, one day, I'll be given a chance to make up for all my short comings as a husband and a father."

Stan took a slightly different route back to the beach to start his coastline search. As soon as he got back into the canopy of the trees; he again, had that odd sensation that "those eyes" were watching him. It left him with an uneasy, kind of creepy feeling. He found a large strong stick that he could use as a staff to help him walk; and if need be, he could use it to defend himself against "the eyes".

On his way down the mountain, Stan discovered a small, clear stream running from somewhere in the mountain toward the sea. He, first, drank all the water he could take in; then he laid in the stream letting the cool water wash over his parched body. What a lovely feeling to have the clean fresh water soothing his sun burnt body and aching muscles. He had not been this relaxed, since he maneuvered his boat away from the dock back in Florida. Florida seemed so long ago, so much had happened. The plans he had made for so much fun were all nothing but a disaster now. He thought he could lie there in the cool water all day; but the shoreline was calling out to him. He had to find out, if there was help for him on this island.

Stan followed the little life-giving stream to a rock outcropping on the shore; where the stream drained its life sustaining waters into the sea.

Stan, again, kidding with himself said, "So that's how the ocean is filled up, right from this little stream."

It was childish thoughts, but it was all he had to keep his mind off the ugly images of being stranded here on this island, and menacing thoughts like "the eyes".

From this point on the island, Stan planned to follow the shoreline around this little piece of "paradise"; until he found help or arrived back at this same spot where he was about to start from. He hoped it would not be the latter. He estimated that it would take him two days to circle the island. But before he left, he thought of a way to take drinking water with him. He could empty the milk from several coconuts and refill them with fresh water. Then, reseal the hole with a tightly rolled leaf that he would force into the opening he had made in the coconut.

He was pleased with his homemade "water bottle", thinking, "I wonder if anyone has a patent on this design, I'll make a mental note of this; 'Stan's Natural Canteen'." He chuckled.

Stan started out on his expedition from the east side of the island heading in a southerly direction. As he moved south, he had not, yet, seen any signs of human life on the island; but he did see crabs on the shore, and a few, what appeared to be, promising fishing spots. He also noted other things that he will need; if he will be here for the long haul.

Stan sighed, "I hope that is not going to be the case." But he remembered the Boy Scout motto, "Be Prepared".

When he neared the southern tip of the island; he noticed a pile of opened oyster shells near the tree line. He went over to investigate. The shell pile told Stan two things: one, there most likely is an oyster bed close by and that would mean an excellent source of food. And even more important, someone or something had to harvest these oysters and leave the shells here. But, again, he could not find any signs of human life; however the shell piles gave Stan new hope.

Stan completed his trip around the island, late the third day, having not seen any sign of human life with the possible exception of the oyster piles. He realized he had completely circled the island when he saw his own footprints in the sand, left days earlier. *This would be the lowest point in Stan's life; when he concluded that he may be the only human inhabitant on this island, and he may be here for a very, very long time.*

He sank to his knees down onto the sand, crying out, *"Why me?"*

Soon enough, he would find out *"Why me?"* And that information would come from a most inconceivable source. But then again, it is said that God works in mysterious ways; and this would prove to be one of those "God only" events.

CHAPTER FOUR

REFLECTIONS ON THE PAST

The following day, Stan sat on the beach feeling sorry for himself; then he started to look back on his life trying to determine where he had gone wrong. He was one of two children to hard working, loving parents who always wanted the best they could afford for their children. His dad was a blue collar worker and his mother was a stay-at-home mom. They sent the children to private schools hoping to give them the best education, in the best environment they could provide. In the process, Stan, his sister and both his parents found Jesus through the grace of God.

Stan's parents grew into strong Christians; his dad even becoming a preacher in his later years. His sister was apparently following in her parents' footsteps; while the parents were maintaining a Christian household for themselves and their children. But after a few years, Stan started drifting from God and rejecting the teachings of his father. Stan's rebellious ways took him into things that a teenage boy should never have been involved in like marijuana, drinking, smoking and some other things that Stan didn't even want to remember. All the while, his dad insisted that Stan go to church every Sunday, while he was living in his father's home. Stan attended church as required; but vowed that he would never go to church again, once he moved out of the family home.

As Stan had promised himself, the day after he graduated from high school; he got a job, an apartment and moved out of his father's house. Without "adult supervision", things only went downhill for Stan. Six months later, Stan joined the army, married, and was on his way to serve his country at war. During his time in the military, Stan matured, and changed a lot of his old ways, but not all of them; and he did not include God in his future plans. Upon discharge from the Army, Stan went into the retail industry and earned a college degree. After rising through the ranks of his company, he was recruited by a Fortune 500 Company. He later retired as a director from that company.

Stan had a good career and he wasn't a bad father; but, he could have been a much better husband and father. He could have spent more time with the family and less time on the job. Financially, the family did well; but there were promises broken along the way, emotional pain that he caused various people, hurts that he wished he could take back, angry words spoken and dreams broken. But for now; he is left alone, on this isolated beach, with memories both good and bad.

He asked himself, "How did I let things get this far out of hand?"

And then, Stan remembered the words that he told his dad about never going to church again. The longer he rebelled against God, the further he removed himself from His presence.

CHAPTER FIVE

MAKING A
NEW HOME

Stan came to the realization that he was going to be on the island for some time, maybe a long, long while. Not only was there no human life on the island, but he had still not even seen a single ship off in the distance. It was as if he, and this island, had been just dropped off in this isolated spot in the middle of this God forsaken ocean. After accepting the reality of his situation, Stan knew he had to have better living conditions for himself. If he wanted to survive for any amount of time; he would have to build a shelter to get out of the rain and weather, and pin point various sources of food. Although the coconuts were a good source of milk and "meat", he could not live off of coconuts alone. He would need protein.

His plan would be to search inland for any fruits and vegetables that he may find growing wild. His main source of protein most likely would have to come from the sea. However, he had seen a few monkeys on the island; but they remained aloof and would be hard to catch. Anytime he would move towards one of them; they would disappear into the thick foliage of the jungle. He had never tasted monkey meat; but he knew that some people in other countries did enjoy monkey as a food source. He had never before thought of eating monkeys;

but under these conditions anything would be possible. Everything would have to be considered as a food source in these circumstances, including bugs, lizards, birds and even monkeys if he could catch one. The first order of business would be to build a shelter to keep himself out of the elements. He planned a simple lean-to made from a framework of sticks he could find along the beach. The frame would be covered with broad leaves he could harvest from plants nearby. He would tie down the leaves to the frame using small vines. Next, he would cover the floor with a thick layer of the same leaves to use as a bed. He decided to locate the shelter near to where the stream came out of the mountains and met the sea. This location would provide a steady source of drinking water close at hand.

Stan resting in camp.

After constructing the lean-to, Stan next gathered stones for a fire pit. He knew he would need a fire for cooking and a large pile of wood close by to light as a signal fire, if he should see a passing ship. The number of matches he had in his survival kit was limited; so, he would have to keep the cooking fire continuously burning and from there he could light the signal fire when, and if, the time came. He prayed that the time would soon come.

Stan also knew that he would need to make some tools for hunting and fishing, but that would have to start tomorrow. For now he would have to go gather more coconuts for dinner. As the days wore on, Stand would have to travel further and further down the beach to find the tasty brown "hairy balls". This afternoon as he walked along the tree line he came upon a tree with eight to ten coconuts laying beneath it on the ground.

He thought, "This is great luck, I haven't seen this many coconuts under one tree since I've been here."

He moved under the tree and begun gathering up his newly found bounty.

Suddenly, from out of the tree top, Stan heard a loud voice, "*Hey dude, what do you think you are doing?* You can't just come on this island and steal a monkey's food, whenever you like!"

Stan fell back into a sitting position on the sand still holding onto the coconuts he had picked up. He sat there in shock with his mouth open looking up into the tree.

The monkey yelled even louder, "*DUDE, DO YOU HEAR ME OR ARE YOU DEAF?*"

Stan still in shock and having not moved, said, "Are YOU talking to me?"

The monkey replied, "No, I'm talking to all the other thieves who are under this tree trying to steal my coconuts! Oh boy, I got a real wise guy on my hands. Not only is he a thief; he's also got a big mouth."

By this time the monkey was scurrying down the tree as fast as he could descend. Stan did not know what to do. Should he run, or prepare to fight off this irate "talking monkey"?

Stan thought, "This must be some kind of weird day dream; monkeys don't talk."

But the next thing he knew, the angry monkey was yelling right into his face. "If this isn't real, my dream monkey has bad breath with a slight hint of banana," thought Stan.

The monkey continued to go on his rampage, "I have a good mind to punch you right is that big fat thing on your face you most likely call a nose. You don't see any of us over there at that flimsy lean-to of yours taking your stuff, *No*, we respect the rights of others. But here you are! You come on our island, uninvited, I might add; and just take it upon yourself to take whatever you want. Well, what have you got to say for yourself? Or are you intelligent enough to respond to me? Answer in a series of grunts, if you have to, *well*?"

All Stan could say is, "You talk!"

The monkey threw up his hands, "You are brilliant, a regular Einstein and Baby Face Nelson all rolled into one big mouth."

Stan still in shock replied, "You really do talk."

Following that comment, the monkey calmed down and sat in the sand across from Stand and said, "Look man I apologize. I'm having a bit of a bad day, today. There is no need to take the coconuts; I would gladly give you all you need."

Stan slowly coming out of shock from meeting an angry, talking monkey, and no longer feeling threatened, also apologized. "I saw your coconuts and assumed they had just fallen to the ground. I did not see you in the tree. I would never steal from you or anyone else."

The monkey said, "Take whatever you need and have a blessed day."

"You can talk!"

Stan took two coconuts and thanked the monkey, but then asked, "Can I ask you a question?"

"Sure," the monkey replied.

"How many of you monkeys are on this island; and if you knew I built that shelter why didn't someone make contact with me before?"

The monkey responded, "Those are reasonable questions. There are about eighty of us here. As far as making contact with you, only a few of the old ones have ever seen a man before. We have had you under surveillance ever since you arrived, but we were not sure of your intentions. We planned to watch you for a while before we approached you; but this chance encounter pretty much negated all that. And some of our little ones were afraid that you would try to eat them. You weren't thinking about anything like that, were you?"

Stan quickly responded, "No, of course not!"

He lied; at least, he wouldn't ever consider such a thing now. How could he eat intelligent beings, monkeys or not? As Stan walked off, he had to pinch himself to make sure he wasn't dreaming.

Stan wondered, "How can this all be true? No one would ever believe I was talking with a monkey. I don't believe it myself, and I was there. And what did the monkey mean by 'have a blessed day'? That couldn't mean what I think it means! No, I cannot believe that the monkey meant for me to have a day that is blessed by God. That's a leap that I'm just not ready to take, talking monkey or not. How would they know about God on this little island?"

Stan turned to look back to where he had just left, there were several young monkeys that came out of the thick vegetation to pick up the dropped coconuts. One of the youngsters was watching Stan; and when he turned to look back, the young monkey waved to him. Stan waved back.

Stan said to himself, "I can't believe that a grown man my age is "waving bye" to a monkey. Where, on God's green earth, did I land? Or in my case, I guess I should say, where in God's blue sea, am I marooned?"

By the time Stan got back to his new "home", the sun had already started to slide behind the island's mountains. Once the sun goes down here, it gets dark very fast. You cannot see much, after sunset, unless there is a bright moon. This will not be one of those bright nights. He would go to bed on his new mattress of leaves and have a lot to think about. He was having a hard time trying to understand what he had seen and heard today.

"Who would ever believe that I was verbally insulted by a monkey who wanted to beat me up, because he thought I was stealing from him? Then, the monkey apologized to me, when he found out there was a misunderstanding between us. And, I, in turn, apologized back to the monkey. Who's going to believe that one? I wouldn't. If I ever get home and repeat this story, I'll be going from the island to the 'Looney Tunes Ward' at the hospital. Surely, the authorities will want to place me into some type of mental health unit for therapy; I couldn't blame them, after hearing a story like mine."

Needless to say, Stan had a restless night following his chance meeting with the monkey in the tree. This has changed everything he had previously known, seen or been taught. This defies all laws of nature as he knew them.

CHAPTER SIX

AN ISLAND DWELLER'S LIFE

Stan woke up early the next morning. He admitted to himself that he will probably be on this island for an extended time. After all, the monkey had said that only a few of the older monkeys had even seen a man before; so Stan concluded that, apparently, the island is not visited very often by people. But that did leave a ray of hope. At least, at some point, they have encountered other humans.

He thought, "I can't believe I'm saying this; but, at least, I have monkeys to talk to." Stan assumed that if one monkey could talk, the rest of the troop could also talk. He was right.

He got out of his bed and prepared to work. The first order of things would be to make some tools for hunting and fishing. Stan would need a long cane to use as a fishing pole. He had seen some that grew along the mountain stream.

As he followed the stream up into the mountain he said to himself, "One of those would do just fine". He added, "I could use another cane, about five feet long, to catch crabs along the water's edge. Now what else will I need? I better get my shopping list made before I drive down to the store; I hope they take VISA or one of my other credit cards here." Stan had to laugh at that, "At least I still have a sense of humor. I'll also need a long hardwood stick I can make into a spear for fishing, and a short stick I can make into a small club using a small rock as a head. Now, where did I put my car keys? Oh, I am a regular comedian." Stan said, laughing to himself.

Stan went out and gathered all the materials he would need to make his tools. While he was at "the store", he picked up some other hardwood sticks that he could use to roast fish over his cooking fire. He returned home, sat down on a rock, and began constructing the tools that will help keep him alive for as long as he is on the island. Stan was busy at work and did not hear the monkeys approach.

He was startled when he heard a voice say "Hello". It was the "tree monkey" accompanied by a smaller monkey.

Stan said, "Hi, I didn't see you coming in."

The tree monkey said, "We got off on a bad start yesterday; and we didn't properly introduce ourselves. They call me 'Tree Top', because I can get up into the top of a tree faster than anyone else in the troop." He said that with pride in his voice. "And this is Skippy. You two have already met but you may not have remembered that first meeting."

"My name is Stan. But I don't remember meeting Skippy. Is he one of the young monkeys who was with you yesterday?"

"No, Skippy was the first one of us to see you. He saw you being carried ashore."

Stan excitedly interrupted, "Wait, wait! I thought I was washed up on shore, alone. Did one of my fishing buddies make it onshore, also? What happened to him? Where is he?" Stan asked, as he grabbed Tree Top by the shoulders.

Tree Top said, "No, it was not one of your buddies." And as he started to explain, Stan again cut him off.

"If Skippy was the first one to see me from your troop and he did not bring me in from the ocean; and it was not one of my buddies, who was it? Who carried me onto the shore?" His last question was directed at Skippy, who was a little intimidated by Stan's excitement and body animation.

Tree Top told Skippy that maybe it would be best if he gave Stan an account of the things that transpired on Stan's first day on the island. Since Skippy was frightened by Stan's demeanor; and, had moved behind Tree Top for protection. Tree Top, now, nudged Skippy to come out from behind his back, to talk to Stan. Skippy then stepped around his protector.

Stan lowered his voice and slowed the tempo of his speech. He, then asked, "Skippy, please tell me what happened and what you saw?"

Skippy was feeling a little more confident, and less intimidated, due to the change in Stan's tone of voice, started his description of the facts. He also felt re-assured because he was being backed up by Tree Top as his protector. "I was playing by myself over by the tree line off the beach where you came ashore. I looked out to sea and saw an angel walking on water carrying something, which turned out to be you. He was wearing a white robe with a golden sash tied around his waist; and there was a bright glow around his head. And, although he came out of the water; he was not wet. The angel walked onshore and laid you down in the sand."

An angel brings Stan ashore.

"After laying you on the sand, the angel called me to come to where you and he were. When I approached the angel, he told me to go get two coconuts and set them beside you. When I returned with the coconuts; the angel nodded his head in approval, then vanished. I, then, ran home to report to our elders what had happened."

Tree Top picked up the story from there. "When Skippy got home, he reported that an angel had brought a white, hairless monkey onto the island. We have all seen angels, but no one had ever seen a white, hairless monkey; so we sent a delegation to check you out. One of the elders, who had once seen a man, went with us. It was he who confirmed; that you are a man and not a monkey. To be honest, most of us were hoping for a monkey. After that, we always had at least one of our troop members watching you. We were warned that some men can be mean and very aggressive. We had to know what kind of man you are, friend or foe, before we could trust you around our families." Then Tree Top point blank asked, "Stan, just what kind of man are you?"

Stan was a little taken back by the forwardness of the question, but he thought, "If I were in their position; I, too, would want to know what kind of person was invading my homeland."

Stan started out, "Well when I was growing up I was a little rough; I liked to fight. I got interested in girls, way too early; and I started drinking and partying in my latter teens. I was determined to do life my own way; not listening to those wiser than myself. I got married, by the time I was twenty years old, and had two kids. I joined the Army, saw war; and then, got into a career field that left me pretty callous toward people in general. Those experiences just reinforced my position on life; 'it's my way or the highway'. I, later, changed careers which allowed me to mellow, somewhat; but the hard partying carried on for a while. In the middle of that crazy lifestyle, I let go of the Christian principles and values that my parents had taught me."

He paused, and then added, "But to be honest with you, since I have arrived here I have had plenty of time to do an evaluation of my life. I have made plenty of mistakes. I did plenty wrongs that should never have happened, and I have caused enough hurt for several life times. I have done all of this; and have no way to make things right, or even just to say I'm sorry."

Stan stopped talking and wondered why he had even told this monkey all his deep dark secrets. It just felt good to talk to someone, anyone. He thought, "Surely, this monkey could not understand the world I came from."

Tree Top waited until Stan went silent, then he put his hand on Stan's shoulder. "My friend, you have a lot of issues to work out, and our island allows time and space for that. I hope that you will take advantage of the wise and deep thinking monkeys in our troop. They are much smarter than I, and they are good at helping others work through their problems."

Stan replied, "I'm open to anything, I have nowhere else to turn."

"Stan you may not believe this, now, and I don't have the answers; but you have been brought here for a reason. We will help you find out what that reason is."

Tree Top interjected, "Before I forget, Skippy and I are the official 'Island Welcome Party'. Our leaders are extending an invitation to a welcoming party being held in your honor, tomorrow, at our place. Should you choose to accept our offer, I will be by in the morning, to escort you to our place of residence." After presenting the "formal invitation" Tree Top added, "It's a come as you are party: no need to dress up. We will be wearing our casual attire." With that, he and Skippy laughed hard at his joke. Stan joined in on the laugh.

As they started to leave, Stan asked, "By the way what is the name of this island?"

In unison they both responded, "Monkey Island, of course!"

Stan watched as they walked away, and thought, "I have seen many monkey islands in various zoos around the country, but none like this one. And not a one of those had talking monkeys. And, now, I'm going to a party hosted by monkeys; unbelievable".

Stan went back to his tool making; but could not get all this new information out of his head. "What about the story of the angel rescuing me from the sea? I believe Skippy saw something, but I don't know if I can believe an angel carried me out of the sea onto dry ground. Even if I believed an angel could do that; why would God send one of His angels to save the likes of me? When I rebelled as a young teen, did all what I did, and sinned like I did for so many years; surely God forgot about me a long time ago. Well, I'll forget about all that for now, tomorrow its party down monkey style," and he laughed.

Stan first made his fishing pole, which was the easiest tool to make. All he had to do was take a section of fishing line from the small roll he found in his survival kit, tie one end to the longest cane pole, and tie the opposite end to one of his two hooks.

When he finished the fishing pole, he thought, "I use to fish for fun. Now I will be fishing for food so I can live; how things have turned around."

Then he was, again, saddened by the thought of his three fishing buddies that were on his boat with him, when it went down. "I hope that they made it to safety; I have to hold onto the thought they made it home alive."

Stan was not a skilled outdoorsman, but he learned a few helpful things from his scouting days; and he had watched nature films and Cowboy and Indian movies "back in the day" to pick up on a few more tricks. He recalled the clubs that the Indians used in some of the old movies, and designed his club in that fashion. He would use a two foot long hardwood stick as the handle, split on one end wide enough to fit a small stone; which was tied into place with strips of inner, soft bark from a tree. The handle, below the stone, was also wrapped tight; so, that the wood would not continue to split further down the shaft.

"That's it, my trusty club!"

Next he would make his "crab fork". To do this he took the shorter of the two cane poles and split one end up about eight inches from the bottom into four sections. Stan used strips of bark to tightly wrap around the cane pole just above the "splits" he had made; this would stop the "spits" from going further up the cane shaft. Stan then took a small rock and jammed it as far up into the split sections as he could. He experimented with different size rocks, until he found the one that would produce the correct size spread at the end- about three inches would be the correct size opening. Once he had the right size rock in place, he secured it there with more strips of bark. He would use the fork to pin a crab to the sand; while holding the crab in place, he could then pick it up with his hand without getting pinched.

"Now there's a 'crab fork' that any man, stranded on an island with talking monkeys, would be proud of." He then placed it in his growing pile of tools.

The hand shovel was made similar to the club using an oyster shell half as the head. And the spear would be made from the six foot hardwood stick by carving the head into a sharp point, leaving a barb on one side that would help hold the prey in place, until he could grab hold of it. He was satisfied with all his works and stood to his feet.

He beat on his chest; like he had seen big apes in the movies do, proclaiming, "I am the best man on Monkey Island." Thinking, "Because I am the only man on the island, or 'hairless white monkey' as Skippy called me," he had to laugh at himself.

Stan went off to catch dinner.

CHAPTER SEVEN

PARTY TIME

Stan recalled the term "as fun as a barrel full of monkeys" and he thought to himself, "I am about to find out just how much fun that really is. I wonder how many people can say they went to a monkey party. Tomorrow I will be able to say 'I partied like a monkey'. When I get back to civilization; I'll make that a slogan and print it on T-shirts- 'Party like a Monkey'. I'll make a million bucks," at that he laughed to himself.

About mid morning Tree Top came by to get Stan to escort him to the monkey cave.

Tree Top said, "We will travel to the northern end of the mountain range which is where we have made our home."

Tree Top could sense that Stan was feeling some apprehension about going into unknown surroundings, and into the middle of a bunch of strange monkeys he does not know. So, Tree Top attempted to put Stan at ease by telling him about their society here on the island.

Tree Top started by outlining the troop structure. "We are led by Maw who is the matriarch of our troop. Maw receives counsel from three of our wisest elders. And then, there are the individual family units made up of a husband, wife and kids. Lastly there is Max; he is our Sergeant at Arms. Max is a pretty scary looking guy and can be tough when need be; but he really is a nice guy once you get to know him. Most of Max's duties revolve around straightening out the young ones when they start to get out of line at group functions. Most likely you will get to see him in action, today.

Everybody is very excited about you coming to meet with us. Some of the very little ones have not even got a look at you yet. That is our simple organization; we do not complicate life here on the island. We are gentle, kind and love one another; and above all we love the Creator."

Monkey Family

Stan didn't know what to say about Tree Top's last comment; so, he changed the subject. "What about you Tree Top, are you married? Do you have any infants?"

"I am married; you will meet my wife today. But we do not have any infants; we are expecting our first in about sixty days. You will learn much about our troop today." With that they walked in silence for a long way.

Stan was thinking about what Tree Top had said about "The Creator" and what Skippy said yesterday about an angel. And then, Tree Top added that they all have seen angels.

He thought, "I'm a college educated man and I don't understand any of this. Is this some kind of extended dream, did I really drown, or am I just going crazy?"

He was still deep in thought, when the silence of the jungle island was broken buy the sound of beating drums.

Tree Top announced, "We are nearing the troop's cave."

Stan was not prepared for what he saw next. They broke through the heavy foliage of the jungle into a large clearing at the foot of a mountain. In front of what was obviously the cave opening, was a large spread of food laid out in banquet style on banana leaves. Off to one side was a group of monkeys playing a tune on a number of different style handmade drums.

Stan thought, "They are harmonizing a pretty good sound; it was obvious the crowd was pleased with the music".

Monkeys everywhere were jumping and dancing to the beat of the drums. Some were wearing party hats made from plant leaves; others were wearing necklaces made of beautiful native flowers. Sitting on a rock above the party goers was what had to be Max, a large silverback gorilla. He was definitely menacing looking, not one you would want to cross.

Max, the Sergeant at Arms.

At the far end of the clearing, Stan saw what appeared to be a cultivated garden. "That can't be," Stan said, as he rubbed his eyes to ensure his vision was clear and he was not seeing something in his imagination. "It is real, alright."

In all, he counted about seventy eight monkeys give or take a few.

And there was something else; near the cave entrance was a fire pit with a burning fire. "I always believed that monkeys were afraid of fire. What next will these guys spring on me," thought Stan?

When the troop noticed that Stan had arrived, the drums quieted. Everyone stopped dancing and talking, and all turned to see "the white hairless monkey".

Maw walked out of the crowd, approached Stan, placed a flower necklace over his head; and then said, "Welcome to our home."

Stan thanked her for their hospitality. The monkeys all cheered; and the party resumed as quickly as it had stopped.

Maw stated, "You just cannot hold this group back from a good party. You must forgive them; it's not often when we have an excuse to throw a party. I know being on our island is not what you planned or want; but let's make the best of it while you are here among us. Please mix in and meet everyone. Tree Top will stay with you to make the introductions. We will eat in about an hour."

She saw the bewildered look on Stan's face and offered this reassurance, "Don't worry; we don't expect you to remember everyone's name, at first. I understand, to you, we all look alike. That's okay; if I went into your world, I would think all of you look alike, too. And please don't mind the infants (all non-adult monkeys). They are very inquisitive; and you are especially interesting to them. Just disregard all their touching.

Remember, most of my troop has never seen a man, before you arrived. I know you have a hundred questions; but today we celebrate your safe, miraculous arrival. Tomorrow, we will have time for questions. For now LET'S PARTY" and with that Maw danced off.

Maw and Stan

As promised, Tree Top stayed with Stan introducing him to monkey after monkey, making small talk as they progressed through the crowd. Stan found them all to be friendly and polite; no one asked where he came from or anything like that. They had to have been very well schooled on what they were allowed to ask.

Stan thought, "If I were them, I would want to know everything about this 'strange being' in their mist. I'm the 'elephant in the room', and everyone is talking around me like there was nothing out of the ordinary. What's up with that?"

After about an hour, a loud trumpet sounded from a monkey with a large sea shell. The drums stopped, and everyone gather around the "banquet table", and all held hands.

Stan thought, "I see this with my own eyes, but I don't believe what I'm seeing. We did this at home when I was growing up. They are about to pray!"

That is exactly what happened. One of the older monkeys lead a prayer thanking God for the food and their guest, and he ended the prayer "In the name of Jesus."

Stan's mind was racing in many different directions at once, "OK, this is impossible! How could monkeys on an isolated island with little to no visitors even know about God and Jesus Christ? How could monkeys be Christians? How could they be better Christians than most of the people I know? I'm going crazy, I know it; somebody call 911? OK, I give up; let me in on the joke."

Tree Top put his arm around Stan's shoulders, "Stan, we know this is all new and strange to you. Tomorrow, Maw will provide you with many of the answers you are looking for; but for now, it's time to eat and enjoy yourself. You have been through a lot."

After the prayer, everyone waited very politely for Stan to take his food before they would serve themselves. Even the infants waited their turn. There was quite a spread laid out before them. At one end of the "table" were oysters on the half shell. On the other end of the table, were roasted lizards on a stick that Stan found to be very tasty. In the center of the table were avocados, bananas and breadfruit. They, also, served cooked eggplant, plantain and calabash; which is a spinach like dish. For a beverage, they served juice made from a berry found on the island. Of course, everything served was from the island; even the garden items were cultivated from wild plants found growing on the island. Gourds were used as cups and bowls. When dried out, they become hard like wood and can be used for food service.

After everyone had eaten their fill, the drums started up, again; but only a few of the hardiest monkeys got up to dance. Most were too full to move. Monkeys were saying their good-byes to Stan and drifting off to find a cool place to take a nap. Stan understood. He, too, was tired and his mind was stressed from everything he had seen and heard, today.

Stan said, "Tree Top I am ready to go home, also."

Tree Top offered, "I'll walk back with you."

Stan declined Tree Top's offer, "I need to be alone to do some serious thinking."

Tree Top said, "Go with the peace of God in you."

Before Stan left what remained of the party, he found Maw; so, that he could thank her for all she had done.

Maw said, "My son, you are troubled, and this is certainly understandable. But you did not find this place out of luck; you were sent here by God. This troop and I were placed in your life and you in ours, because God meant it to be that way. Nothing in His world happens by chance. You have much soul searching to do. You have much to learn and many decisions to make. I don't know if anyone has told you, but God has blessed me with the responsibility of being one of His prophets. I prophesied long before you got here, that you would come. I will be your spiritual guide while you are here among us. Go home, now, and try to get some rest; come back to the cave in the morning. I have been praying for you Stan. I will continue to do so, until God delivers you."

Stan was so overwhelmed he did not say a thing; he didn't know what to say. He walked away with many more questions than answers.

CHAPTER EIGHT

COME TO THE MOUNTIAN

The next morning, Stan woke up early after thinking all night about the "party". He had a whole laundry list of questions he wanted to ask Maw. He was glad she had invited him back. Stan ate the leftovers that Tree Top's wife had packed for him, before he left the party yesterday. It may not have been a gourmet meal, but it was good and there was certainly plenty of food. As soon as he finished eating, he washed up and headed back out for the mountain cave.

When Stan arrived at the cave clearing, he noticed how clean the area was. All signs of the party were gone, and the grounds had been "policed up". Monkeys were going about their chores. Workers were tending the garden, and the infants were playing. He did not see Tree Top anywhere. Several monkeys waved to him but continued doing whatever they were working on. A few of the infants did run up to greet Stan.

He thought, "At least they no longer think I want to eat them; I will never admit what I was thinking just a few days ago."

When Maw saw Stan standing in the clearing; she called, "Come over here and sit with me."

After he was escorted over to Maw by the infants; she shooed the young ones away. "Stan, sit down, and relax, so that we may talk. You must have a million questions you want to ask, and this is your time to do so."

He burst out with so many different things; she said, "Stop, stop, you are talking so fast, I can hardly understand you. Now, let's start over and go slow this time. We have all day, all week, and however long it takes. That is unless you have some other place you have to be." She chuckled at her little joke.

Stan apologized, "Maw, I'm sorry. Thank you for taking time with me. There is so much I want to ask. Let me start with this: I have heard several of your troops members mention that there was at least one other man on this Island. When was that, and what happened to him?"

Maw answered, "He was on the island about twenty five years ago."

Stan's follow-up questions were, "And what happened to him? Did he get off the island?"

Maw waited about a minute before she responded; then in her slow easy going style told Stan, "Many of the monkeys that are here now were not, yet, born when the man arrived on our shores. So, the younger ones have only heard about him through stories handed down by our elders. When we saw him come ashore; we made contact with him. We honored him with a party, just like we did for you. Following the party, we invited him back the next day for dinner, just like I asked you here today," and she then paused.

But before she could start back up with the story; Stan broke in, "What happened next?"

"Slow down son, we are on 'island time' here. Everything is at a slow-pace, no rush."

Stan said. "Sorry" and she went on with the story.

"Well, we were talking, and everything was going fine until right before dinner." She, again, paused and looked at Stan, then went on. "He was okay with everything; until we asked *him* to step into the 'boiling pot'. It was then that he realized *he was going to be dinner.*"

Maw, then, stared right into Stan's eyes and waited for his reaction. Stan scooted back in utter fright. Wide eyed, he looked around to see if they were coming for him. Maw broke the tension with roaring laughter. She rolled on her back laughing so hard she could not contain herself.

"I'm just kidding, I'm kidding; and you should have seen your face. No, no we would never boil a man; we much prefer you all roasted."

Stan, for a second time, snapped his head around looking in all directions; then back toward Maw. She laughed all the harder, again, rolling on the ground.

"WHAT'S FOR DINNER!"

Maw regained her composure, and Stan finally relaxed, after Maw reassured him that she was just having a little fun with him.

"You have to forgive me, I've been waiting twenty five years to tell that one, and it was worth the wait. The look on your face was priceless," and she started laughing all over again. Then, after settling down again, she said, "By the way, did you hear the one where a man was lost in the jungle, when he saw a monkey up in a tree. He stopped at the base of the tree and called up to the monkey, 'Do you live in this area?' The monkey said, 'No I'm just hanging around.' Do you get it? He was hanging in the tree? It's monkey humor, Stan; that's funny stuff. Lighten up son, lighten up," and, again, she was laughing hard.

Serious now she asked, "Okay, where do you want to start? And how can I help you better understand your situation?"

Stan replied, "To be honest, I have never heard monkeys speak, how did that happen? How did the troop get on this island? Where do you get your information from? It appears that you all know a lot more than just what is happening on the island. Do you have a connection to the outside world beyond these shores? And I don't want this to sound rude; but, how do you know so much about God?"

"Well Stan, those are all very good questions. I certainly understand why you would want to get answers to these issues. None of these topics call for a simple yes/no answer. Some are going to require lengthy explanations; so, let's take them one at a time."

Maw started to fill Stan in as best she could, "Monkeys have always had a verbal language. In fact, this is really going to set you back on your heels; all animals communicate the same way. And your response is you never heard any of us speak before; that can't be. The problem with you humans is that none of you ever take the time to learn from us. As a race, you are self centered and think you are superior to all the other spices on earth. Now granted, God did give man the responsibility to have dominion over all things on earth, and the authority to name the animals; I give you that. But that didn't mean we were not given any intelligence in our own right."

"My son, you are a perfect example of what I speak. And how did you take time to learn about us? You came to our shores half dead, and because there is nowhere else to turn, there is nothing else you can do; you come to us for help and answers. No problem, that is what we are required to do; help our neighbor out. People treat us like an animal; that is why we act that way. And, as soon as, someone learns that one of us can talk; they make millions of dollars off of us by forcing us to act in movies and television commercials; I know you have seen them. Word travels fast in our world! Is it not true that, most people make fun of monkeys," Maw asked.

Stan didn't want to lie to his host, especially when she apparently already knew the answer, so reluctantly he said, "Yes".

"Yes, people stereotype us; they say we are all one of three kinds: "Monkey see no evil, monkey speak no evil or monkey say no evil. Well, I'm sure your time on the island has already proven that theory wrong."

Stan shook his head in the affirmative.

"Not all monkeys, but, here, we try to look for the good in others. We only listen to good, and we try to only speak well of others. And this is the message that we teach our infants.

This brings me to your next question, We learn what is going on around our region through the birds that pass through and stop to rest on our island. You would be surprised at the amount of news and gossip we pickup from those chatty little fellows."

Stan had been taking in every bit of information Maw was putting out. He had already gotten over the shock, and was ready to accept whatever he was told. He concluded that he would have to relearn all that he had already learned in life; and what he would have considered as bazaar, he would, now have to consider as the norm.

For the first time, since Maw started speaking, Stan interrupted, "Excuse me; but are you telling me, you all talk with birds? Let me get this straight in my mind. Am I to understand that these birds fly here with information and news to report to you guys?"

Maw, picking back up on the conversation said, "No not exactly. However, we do communicate together. Why wouldn't we? Basically, birds are our only visitors on the island; so, it is natural that we talk together. Birds don't come here for the sole purpose of providing us with news from the outside world. But they are talkative little feathered friends. All we have to do is listen; they provide all we need to know. Much of what comes from them is through the songs they like to sing."

"Maw, I desperately need to know one more thing. What happened to the man who came to the island twenty five years ago? Was he rescued or did he leave the island?"

Maw replied, "I hate to have to report this to you; but he did not make it off the island alive. When he 'landed' on the island; he, like you, had been in a boating accident. He was in fair physical condition; but, mentally, he just could not get it together, even though we tried very hard to help him. We tried to break through his mental cloud; but we just could not reach him. After only several weeks on the island, some members of the troop saw him swimming out to sea never to be seen again."

Maw and Stan had been talking, ever since he had arrived at the home site. They sometimes walked around the area while they talked, with Maw doing most of the talking. Occasionally, they set down for a drink; and let Maw give her throat a break. They stopped for a lunch of bananas and avocados, and then picked back up on Stan's island education.

Well before the sun had set, Maw told Stan that he should head for home, before it got too dark. She called one of the infants over and had her go get Stan a couple of bananas for the trip home. Handing the fruit to Stan, she told him to return the following day; and she would give him a history lesson on the occupation of the island. Stan thanked Maw and, then, the infant for the bananas and headed out to the beach.

As Stan walked along the beach towards his lean-to; he tried to digest all this new data he had taken in, today. His whole world has been turned upside down; many things he thought he knew about the animal kingdom were wrong and had to be reorganized within his brain. And what about the world he left behind? Stan thought about his family and wondered if they had given up hope on him. He could not blame them. By now they most likely feared the worst, that he had been lost at sea along with the boat. But, just maybe, his fishing buddies who were also on the boat made it to safety. They were all releasing the life raft, when the explosion occurred. If they were able get into the raft, they may have been rescued. But either way, any search for him would have been called off some time ago.

"Anyway, thinking about those things, now, is not going to do me any good while I'm stranded here on this island. This island is definitely different from any other place on earth that I have seen or read about. There is no doubt; this is a special island. I got on the island, and somewhere on this island is the key to me getting off." Stan continued talking to himself as he walked home along the shoreline; his hope had been restored. As Stan walked on the beach, he noticed a number of crabs scooting over the sand. He began to get hungry. It was very late in the afternoon by the time Stan reached the lean-to. He grabbed his "crab fork" determined to have a crab dinner tonight. Stan "penned" three crabs, plenty for a meal, and headed back to the camp. He stoked the coals to bring the fire back to life, and, then, added more kindling and wood to get it hotter. After cooking the crabs he had caught just minutes ago, he ate and fell to sleep on his bed of leaves.

CHAPTER NINE

ISLAND HISTORY

S tan arrived early the next morning at the "monkey
cave" eager to meet with Maw and learn more about
this mysterious island. As he broke through the jungle
vegetation at the camp, he saw everyone going about their
chores as usual. Then, he spotted Maw seated near the cave
entrance with a number of infants in front of her forming a half
circle. When Maw saw Stan, she motioned him over to where
they were all seated. Two of the infants jumped up and ran to
meet Stan. They each took one of his hands and started happily
pulling him back to the semicircle and Maw.

"Good morning Stan, I'm glad you could make it back over,
today, to continue our discussion from yesterday. As you can
see, the infants are also happy to see you; more will be joining
us shortly. When the others learned that I would be telling you
about our history, today, many of them asked if it would be
alright if they too, came and listened to the stories. I was sure
you would not mind," said Maw.

"Of course not," Stan replied. "I'm just so glad that you all
are willing to share something as personal as this with me."

As other members of the troop were still coming, Stan sat
among those who had already arrived. Both young and old
came to hear the story that Maw was about to tell. As everyone
was settling in, Maw explained to Stan that their historical

story in not often told; that is why so many want to hear how it all happened. Just about everyone had found their spot to sit, when one of the smallest monkeys came and sat in Stan's lap. He looked down and smiled at the youngster as she, Debra, was smiling up at him.

Once everyone was seated, some of the anxious little ones started calling for Maw to "please start the story".

Stan remembered that, throughout time, this is how many societies that do not have a written language, passed their history and culture from one generation to the next. He, too, was ready for Maw to get started.

9.1 Captivity

"All of our ancestors came from various homelands, where they enjoyed the freedom of 'the wild' and were able to roam where ever they pleased. Like here they lived in troops with family and friends; but, unlike here, each troop was made up of just one species. However, life was far from tranquil in those days. During those times they had to be constantly on the look-out for predators that would have loved to make a meal of us. It didn't matter if you were young or old, not even the infants were safe. They would eat whatever they could catch. They would take one or two of us, or as many as they could catch. From the lions, tigers, crocodiles, wild dogs, big snakes and people, to them we all tasted the same. Most of the time, they would only kill what the predators could eat right then and there; but not the humans, they would take as many of us as they could and carry the bodies back to their own villages. Many times, our ancestors could only sit high up in the trees and helplessly watch these atrocities occur against their loved ones. They were helpless to defend themselves against their enemies, in those days."

Maw saw the reaction she was getting among some of her listeners and told Debra not to worry; Stan was not like those men. Debra looked up into Stan's face, again, but this time she was not smiling. She was looking for reassurance. Stan smiled, gave her a hug and stroked her little back; she then settled back down and waited for Maw to continue with the story.

After the infants got over the initial shock of their own kind being a food source for so many predators, and, here, hundreds of years later, one of "those predators" is sitting among them; they were ready to hear more of the story.

Maw picked back up on her dialogue, "The times were sometimes hard, and at times, bad things happened; but none of that compared to what was going to come next." She paused while everyone mulled over her last statement. "About 250 years ago, men from far away invaded our home land and captured every monkey they could get their hands on. They took the big apes down to the small spider monkeys.

They had brought with them cages that could 'accommodate' from one to four monkeys depending on their size. As our ancestors were caught, they were forced into the cages and locked down. Once they had filled all the cages they had brought with them, they built more cages. It looked as if these bad men were on a mission to imprison the whole monkey nation. At this point, no one knew why they were doing this horrible thing. The bad men that came to hunt us, before, came to kill and take us away for food; but these men were using large nets and ropes to catch us alive and lock us in cages. They hunted us down to the point where no more of us could be found. All of our ancestors had either been caught or escaped to somewhere deep in the far-a-way jungle.

When the men had finished ravishing our land by capturing all the monkeys they could find; they started bringing the cages to the beach. The beach was just a staging area; from there they put us in small boats and transported us to several large, sailing vessels which were anchored off shore in a protected harbor. Once we arrived onboard, we saw that our homeland was not the only place these evil people had caused disaster. The ship's cargo holes were already full of monkeys; so, the cages that would be our prison cells were to be lashed to the decks along with some other cages that were already there. There were about 500 monkeys in all on this one ship.

The cages were stacked two and three high all over the entire ship's deck. Our relatives and the others would be left out in the weather: in the rain and hot sun. And to make matters worse, if that was possible; they learned what their intended destiny was to be. They all were going to be taken to large plantations in the Caribbean Islands where they were going to be sold into slavery. They would, then, be forced to harvest fruit and vegetables in the fields and orchards. They were coming from a free society, to one of control and forced labor, where they would have poor living conditions. Most families had already been torn apart, and those few families that somehow were able to stay together would most likely be sold separately. They were told these things from the first monkeys who were already on the ship, when our ancestors came aboard. Those first monkeys got their information by listening to the ship's sailors talk among themselves. And when they thought that things could not get any worst, it did.

9.2 A Storm at Sea

"After all the cages had been loaded aboard the ship; the Captain, who was a large, dirty man with a long, black beard came on deck and called for the anchor to be hoisted and the sails set. There wasn't any 'good cage' to be in. The ones on the top got the most breezes, but they also got more of the blistering sun. Being in the bottom cages was 'no picnic' either; you can imagine what fell on those poor guys."

After Maw laid out that tidbit of information, all the infants in the listening audience made comments like "yuck" and "disgusting" in revolt to what they pictured in their minds.

Debra just buried her face in Stan's stomach as he held her tightly, reassuring her that she is protected from such things. Maw, having anticipated this reaction, waited for the little ones to regain their composure. This was not the first time she had told this story. She, too, was little when she first heard the story from an old monkey who was no longer with them. And some day, after Maw is gone, one of these youngsters will be passing on the story to the next generation. Who knows; Debra may be the one called to lead the troop? Only time will tell!

Maw moved on with her historical account of their ancestor's misfortunes; "Needless to say, the conditions on deck were horrible and only worsened with each passing day: sun, rain, cold nights and sea sickness were reeking havoc among all the monkeys. Many were sick with little water to drink and even less food to eat. Things were bad, but then there would be a turn for the worst. The wind stood still; the sails hung limp, and the ships were 'dead in the water'. For several weeks the ships just drifted at the will of the sea current. Food and water were in short supply. The ship's crew was on edge. Tempers were short; and fights were breaking out, all over the ship, among the sailors. The monkeys were the first to feel the supply 'pinch'. Their already meager food rations were cut in half, and then again, until there was nothing at all. Finally their water supply was reduced to two sips a day. Surely this would be the lowest point of their lives; but no, it was not. The sailors, who had also run out of food, started pulling monkeys from the cages to be killed, cooked and eaten. All of this was done on deck, while the remaining monkeys were forced to watch this barbaric spectacle."

Maw told the story with such emotion, that those listening felt like they were there feeling the same pain and terror as their ancestors had so many years ago.

"Every monkey wanted nothing more than to be released from his or her cell; but, now release from their prison cages meant certain death at the hands of these crazed sailors. 'Relief', if you will, came in a most unusual way; the same unpredictable sea that had set their ship adrift for weeks, suddenly awoke from its somber sleep. And it came to life with a fury; the windless skies and the flat seas turned into a different kind of nightmare, in the course of just one hour. Now, the ship was being tossed around like a twig going through white water rapids. This new storm was relentless and unforgiving with waves forty feet high. The ship's main mast was snapped in half like it was no more than a piece of broom straw. When it came crashing down, it tore out the helm smashing sailors and monkey's alike. Now, without any hope what-so-ever of controlling the vessel, they were all at the mercy of the wind and sea.

For two days and nights, the ship was tossed to and fro by the furious sea; anything that was not securely tied down was washed overboard including men and any monkeys that happened to have been broken out from their cages by flying debris. Finally, the ship that our ancestors were in couldn't hold itself together any longer. And as it broke apart, most onboard was sent to a watery grave. Ironically, the wooden cages that were designed to rob the monkeys of their freedom ended up being the salvation for some. Some of the wooden cages held together and floated when they were thrust into the rough seas. Unfortunately, the monkeys in the bottom cages were drowned; but those on the top cages were able to stick their heads up between the bars and 'grab' air between waves. The wind and waves continued to push our ancestors and what was left of the ship onto the reef surrounding this island; the island that would later be named 'Monkey Island'.

The wave action rammed the 'life rafts' and 'coffins' (depending if you were in a top or bottom cage) into the reef breaking them apart, at last freeing the monkeys. The next morning, a gentle breeze was blowing, and the sea was once again calm. But the pristine beech on the west side of the island, that we enjoy today, looked like a war zone, that day. The white sands were littered with the dead, the dying, the injured, the sick and the few survivors. In all only seventy monkeys and five men made it to the safety of the island and lived; all the rest perished. Before you ask, it is unknown what happened to any of the other ships, their crews or the monkeys onboard."

9.3 Island Occupation

"After a couple of days recovering on the beach, the survivors started pulling themselves together. They organized into work parties to clear the beach of bodies and send out search parties to explore the island. By this time, the men among them were well aware that the monkeys could talk. At first, they were just as shocked as our friend Stan was when he first learned that we could talk. Because the men were greatly outnumbered by the monkeys, they were very leery of the situation in which they now found themselves. A few weeks prior, these men were among those who had imprisoned the monkeys; and, then, killed and ate their flesh. Now, they were at the mercy of those same monkeys.

But here on this 'new island' the monkeys clearly had the advantage over their former captors. They not only greatly outnumber the sailors; they knew how to live off the land. Our kind had survived in the wild for thousands of years. And there was one more thing; something that, unknowingly, the sailors themselves had taught the monkeys. The monkeys watched and learned how to fight and how to defend themselves. The sailors did not have the survival skills that would be needed for long term living in an uninhabited environment. The monkeys did; and now they had developed 'battle skills' to add to their abilities.

During these first weeks on the island together, it was obvious that the monkeys were dividing themselves into two separate groups. Our ancestors from the mother land stayed together with a few others who chose to join them. They would go to the north end of the island. There were twenty four monkeys in our group, at that time. The remaining forty six monkeys would live on the south end of the island. A delegation from each of the newly formed monkey troops met with the five sailors. Their mission was to inform the sailors of what the new living conditions were going to be on their new island home.

The men were told that they were to stay in the middle of the island between the two troops of monkeys; that is, if they wanted their lives to be spared. Land boundaries were established. The men were given strict rules to follow, if they hoped to co-exist on the island with the monkeys. Of course, they were given the opportunity to leave, if they chose to swim out to sea. None did.

The rules were few and simple:

1. Stay within the boundaries of your assigned area, and
2. Don't hunt, kill or eat monkeys.

The penalty for violating either of these rules would be immediate death! The sailors were in no position to argue or even try to negotiate a better deal. They were greatly outnumbered, and all things considered, they were getting a pretty good deal. Especially, when you think about what they had done, when they had the upper hand over the monkeys. What they didn't know was that many of the monkeys wanted to take revenge right then and there; but cooler heads prevailed."

Maw explained that all these surviving monkeys had witnessed horrific acts of violence against monkeys; and they had all been victims of ruthless crimes.

She said, "But those who find themselves in these situations, in similar circumstances or even in conditions that may not be as dramatic as what our ancestors had to go through; all have to make a decision in life. Do we go and repeat the same acts that were committed against us, or do we break the chain and rise above it all? Our ancestors chose to climb to a higher level of life than that.

9.4 Early Island Life

"The five surviving sailors did not fair-out very well on the island. The first sailor died within weeks of coming ashore; he passed away from injures he obtained during the ordeal at sea. Another one of the five died at the hand of his 'friend' in a fight;

that left three. They may or may not have been good sailors at sea; but, their 'sea worthy' legs did not serve them very well on the island. Nor were they any good at functioning in a regular community setting without a 'Captain' to tell them what to do. Like the old saying goes, 'two men are company, but three men are a crowd.' Two sailors teamed up against the third; no one knows what happened to the 'odd man out'. He just vanished from the face of the earth; the monkeys assumed he died at the hands of his two 'friends'. And then there were just two!

The two remaining men grew tired of eating wild bananas and coconuts. They were also growing tired of each other's company, and being confined to a relatively small area on this small island. 'Just who do those monkeys think they are? They can't tell us what to do', the men were heard to have said. The men became braver and braver, and soon started venturing out past the set boundary lines.

On one of these trips into the southern section of the island, they came across two infants playing alone in the jungle. They tried to catch the two infants who narrowly escaped the sailor's trap. The young monkeys ran back to the troop, and excitedly reported what had happened to them in the jungle. Well, there wasn't any calming down the Southern Troop after the near loss of two members of their troop. The men had violated the agreement in the most egregious way; they intended to kill and eat our youth! This action could not and would not be tolerated.

None of the monkeys really trusted the men anyway; they all had witnessed what these people were capable of. There was no debate on what was to happen to the two remaining sailors. They were told the rules right up front, and they knew the penalty for breaking them. 'You will live by the rules, or you will die by the rules'. All the monkeys remembered what had happened to them in the recent past at the hands of these same men and their friends. Now this outrageous act almost happened again. The monkeys wanted revenge, and they wanted blood, *now*! The whole troop hunted down the men, and the sentence was carried out swiftly. Now, the island was truly 'Monkey Island' with monkeys being the only mammals on this tiny island nation from sea to shining sea."

9.5 Two Troops, One Island

"Although monkeys obviously ruled the island since they were the only inhabitants; there were two totally different styles of 'government' being applied on the island. In the south, a pure dictatorship was established; the strongest monkey became the leader. Everyone else did as he said, or pay the consequences and then be forced to do as they were told. In this troop, only the strongest had a voice; all others were required to 'shut up' and follow orders. This was a non-inclusive troop. All the monkeys were of the same breed, no one else was allowed to be a part of their troop.

A totally different thing was happening in the North. A diverse troop was made up of all the 'leftover' monkeys on the island. They came together to develop what would be a simple democratic organization, where they elected Mother as the first matriarch of the troop. Three elders were selected to provide Mother counseling. Then, they chose a Sergeant-At-Arms to keep the order in the troop when necessary. The guiding principles were that everyone was created equal and is to be respected no matter their breed, color or where they came from. We would all live together and share all things. We would all defend the troop; but fighting among ourselves was not acceptable. All disagreements were to be taken to Mother for resolution. The family unit was placed high on the list of priorities with the union between a male and female; it is to be considered a sacred institution and respected by everyone. The troop still follows these same principles and organizational structure, today.

Another major difference between the North and South troops was their day to day life styles. The Southern Troop was a hunter/gather group. They took whatever they wanted from the land, but never gave back. Our ancestors in the north also hunted and gathered on the island. But, early on, they also realized the island's natural resources would soon be depleted at the rate the two troops were stripping the small jungle of what food sources were available. To ensure that there would be food for the future; our forefathers turned to cultivating and farming to supplement our troop's needs.

Our ancestors were wise to salvage some basic hand tools from the ship wreckage that had been deposited on the island's reef; many of those same tools, we still use today. Some of the monkeys had observed the natives farming in our homeland and they brought that knowledge into the troop. Over time we were able to develop this lovely plantation that continues to provide our troop with food, today. We tried to share our farming techniques with the southern group, but they would not have any part of it. Working the land was below their dignity; they laughed at what our ancestors were doing. They were told, 'Go home and scratch in the dirt like the chickens you are'.

Maw continued her oral history, "Under their dictatorship style of government, life in the south was hard for many; over time, the natural food sources in their area was decreasing due to the increasing population and over harvesting. A few of them started sneaking off to join our troop in the north.

After a few had made their escape, the southern leader threatened to have anyone who was caught trying to 'go north' killed. After about three years of guarded tolerance between the two groups, things were about to come to a head. Relationships were going from bad to worse; the situation was forming up to become a classic 'good vs. evil' conflict. The battle would be between the good monkeys of the North and the monkeys of the South led by the evil dictator."

9.6 The War and The Angel

"The balance of power was with the South, at least in monkey numbers; but our troop did increase some due to southern monkeys deflecting to the North to escape tyranny for a moral and free society. The two troops could no longer coexist side by side on this small island. The South's aggressive actions pushed against the North's passive limits. There were frequent invasions of the northern area by the southern monkeys, where they would take what they wanted from us and our land. Our representatives met in protest with the North's leader but he only laughed in their faces.

Our elders met several times among themselves, but could not come up with a consensus on how to resolve the issue. Understandably, some wanted to fight back, while others wanted to 'turn the other cheek' to keep an all out war from breaking out on the island. However, the overall ecological system of the island was being strained due to over hunting and harvesting. The only thing holding up the North was the plantation; but even that was about to come under attack.

Late one evening the southern troop attacked our camp and plantation. Our ancestors were caught off guard; many

The North vs. The South

When the troop elders met this time, there wasn't any division in their approach to the problem. Even though we were outnumbered, there would be war! There was no other way. Before their meeting was concluded, an Angel of the Lord appeared among them. None had ever seen an angel before this occurrence. They were very much afraid; however, the angel explained who he was and not to fear him."

"The angel said, 'I have been sent by God; who had been watching from heaven what has been taking place on the island. You all are God's creations. God has had His hand on this troop from the time He rescued you from the sea, and placed you all on this island. It was He who stopped the sea wind; then restarted the winds, again, and churned up the sea. It was He who blew the ship against the island reef, causing it to breakup and you monkeys to ultimately land here.

The angel continued, 'Even though you do not know God, you have recognized the Creator. You all live by good morals, love your fellow beings, and understand the union of marriage between a male and a female. We have seen the evil building at the other end of the island, and your resistance to letting evil spread. All the while, you are willing to take in and protect those who flee from the South.'

He went on to say, 'The Lord has chosen this troop. He will come to your aid and fight your battles, as long as you obey Him and accept Him as Master.'

"Then, the angel said", 'Mother, gather the whole troop together and tell them the words that I have spoken, today, to you and this delegation. After you have communicated to the troop, tomorrow morning at dawn, come alone to meet me on that mountaintop.' He pointed to the highest peak on the island. With that said, the angel vanished from among them.

"Mother did as the angel had instructed, telling everyone what had happened. And those who were also in the meeting, with the angel, gave testimony of what they had seen and heard. All were excited, and frightened at the same time; no one had ever seen or heard anything like this before.

Early the next morning, before sunrise, Mother began her climb to the mountaintop. Right at dawn, she made it to the crest where she saw the angel standing on a rock. His eyes were closed, his head was bowed. His arms raised toward heaven.

Mother fell to her knees before the angel, but the angel said,"

'No! Do not worship me; rise up from your knees. I, like you, have been created to worship God, not to be worshipped. Only God is worthy to be worshipped!

Long ago, God chose the Israelites to be His people, and He delivered them out of bondage into a promised land flowing with milk and honey. As God's people, they would have to follow Him and obey His commandments. They could put no other gods before Him. He was faithful to them. He kept His word; He always keeps His word because He is truth.

However, the Kingdom is not just for the Israelites; it is open to anyone who is willing to accept His son, Jesus Christ as Lord and Savior.'

"The angel went on to say," 'I have been sent here to deliver you, and your troop, from the evil one in the south. Then, I will teach you the ways of the Lord. But first, we will rid the island of your enemies. Down to the last evil one must be eradicated; so, that the evil seed does not enter your bloodline. The battle will be done in such a way that all will say, 'The Lord has truly delivered us today.'

'Then I will bring the Word of God to you and instruct you in the ways of our Lord. Now, Mother, depart from this mountain. I will meet with you and your troop, again in two days. You must quickly carry out all the things that you have been told.'

"After two days, the angel reappeared at the troop's camp. He instructed them on the battle plan."

'On the day of the battle, all infants are to be rounded up and left in the cave with the oldest one in charge. They are to remain there until your return. All the adults are to do exactly as I say. Today, each adult is to go out into the jungle and find four big coconuts. Also, each one is to cut two vines three foot long, each strong enough to carry the weight of two coconuts; and harvest a five foot heavy cane. Once they have gathered all these things, then everyone is to return home, and rest through the night.'

'Tomorrow at mid afternoon, all adults will meet in a circle in front of the cave. Each will bring with him all the things that they had collected the day before. Nothing else is to be taken into the circle with the exception of four knives. Once the circle is formed there is to be no talking; the knives will be passed from one to another and a single hole drilled into each coconut at the 'eye'. After all four coconuts have been drilled; each monkey is to drink all the milk from two of his coconuts. He is to drink only half the milk from his third coconut; then, pass it to the monkey on his right who will finish drinking the milk from that coconut. The milk from his forth coconut is to be poured over the hands and feet of the monkey on his left to cleanse them of all dirt.'

'Now a second hole will be bored into an eye of each coconut adjacent to the first hole. Using the vines, one coconut is to be tied to each end making two sets of coconuts for each monkey. One set of coconut is to be carried over each shoulder; so, that the coconuts do not "clang together" when you are walking. The heavy cane is to be carried in the right hand of each monkey.'

'When all preparations have been completed you will quietly walk, again without talking, in single file behind the Sergeant at Arms, on the beach next to the tree line, south toward the enemy's camp. When the troop gets within two miles of the southern camp, you are to move into the jungle and rest. Before dawn, the troop is to quietly move to within thirty yards of the enemy camp. Then, spread out ten yards apart in a straight line. Fifteen minutes before dawn, Sergeant will give the signal; upon his command everyone is to yell 'For the Glory of God', take one step forward while clanging all of the coconuts together. This is to be repeated over and over again until you all reach the edge of the jungle at the camp. At that point, Sergeant is to give the command to attack; and then everyone is to drop their coconuts and charge with their canes, while at the same time, screaming out their loudest war cry. The enemy is to be chased down all the way to the sea, not allowing even one to escape.'

The troop moves into position for battle.

Maw reported, "The troop's movement went with military precision; Sergeant called for the attack and the battle was proceeding as planned. As they broke into the clearing, they could see that the Angel of the Lord was leading the battle and the camp was already abandoned. They chased the southern troop all the way to the sea; but by the time they reached the shoreline the enemy had already run out into the sea and drowned. None were left alive, not one! And the northern troop did not have to strike down not even one monkey; they obeyed, and the Lord fought their battle. All saw that it was the Lord who delivered to them the victory that day. The island was now in the hands of the Lord's monkeys."

By this time Maw was exhausted and her voice sore from the long story telling. She told everyone that she would finish the story tomorrow, but for now she was going to rest. The infants had sat quietly all day, except for a short break at lunch time. When Maw had finished speaking for the day and dismissed the group, everyone was pretty solemn, not talking much. All kept their thoughts to themselves as they made their way back to their own spaces. The monkeys were thinking about what their ancestors had to endure. The young ones who had never seen an angel were trying to imagine what they must look like. And then, there was Stan who had no choice but to keep his thoughts to himself; there was no one else to run his ideas by.

Maw knew that Stan was struggling with all that he had heard; but she thought that it would be best if he first tried to sort things out on his own; there would be plenty of time later to talk.

9.7 Recovery

After the first "history lesson", Maw had told everyone to come back the following day at mid morning to hear "the rest of the story".

Everyone had come early, including Stan; they were all seated and waiting for Maw to join them. Debra was, again, nestled in Stan's lap. They all were anxious to hear what happened after the battle. Maw arrived, and seeing the anticipation on all the faces, she started right back into the story.

"Following the battle all the adults were jubilant. They were giving 'high fives' and congratulating each other about winning the battle without having to fight. The angel, who was still with them, heard their talk of victory and quickly brought them back to reality.

'From heaven we often see this type of behavior among humans. They quickly forget what God has done for them, and are ready to claim credit for themselves. They want to think that they came through the hardship on their own, using their own resources. This reaction becomes their downfall! Now, this troop was victorious in battle, not because of your great military power; in fact, your enemies were stronger than you. And not because you were many in number; they greatly out-numbered you. Your victory was due to your obedience to God. And from this day forward, down through the generations to come, all are to know it was God who fought for you; and it was God who won the battle.'

'God had placed fear in the hearts of your
enemies when they heard the deafening sound
of the coconuts clanging together, and your
small group shouting "Glory to God". However,
they heard what they thought was an army of
hundreds coming through the jungle into their
camp. Their own fear made them run into the
sea, where they drowned as they tried to escape
the "huge army" that was sure to crush them.
God must be given the glory for this victory; He
must be given the honor and thanksgiving for
what He has done here today.'

After a brief pause, Maw went on with the story. "The troop
marched back home singing and praising God. Back at the
camp a big feast was prepared, and the story told and retold to
the infants. The angel did not participate in the festivities, but
he did promise to return and teach the troop in the ways of the
Lord. But, before the angel departed, he taught our ancestors
how to pray to God; which we still do today.

Over the years the angel has reappeared to our troop many
times teaching us about God and introducing us to the Bible.
The Bible that we were given by the angel remains to this day
on the big rock in our cave. With the Bible, the angel brought
the gifts of reading and teaching to several of our elders, along
with the responsibility to pass these gifts on to the generations
to follow. If you look at our Bible; you will see that it is well
used, but not worn out. A Bible that is that well used, over that
long period of time, and has not worn out, is a miracle in itself.

The angel has taught us many things over the years since
his first visit here on the island. And what he has taught us
is as applicable today as it was for the Israelites, and then the

early Church over 2000 years ago. It applies to all who are on this island, and to those beyond our shores everywhere else in the world. Among the most important things that he showed us, was that we need to truly find God; and that we would have to seek for Him ourselves. The angel said that if we seek God; He promised that we *will* find Him, as it is written in the Bible. Then he told us about Jesus Christ, the cross, and what happened on that dreadful and glorious day. Most important of all, the angel explained that we are all sinners and have fallen short of the glory of God. He told us how our sins could be washed away if one believes on Jesus Christ, and he will have everlasting life. Yes, as good as things are on this island, heaven is a much better place. And heaven will last for eternity. It will be an eternity where we will be with our Lord and Savior.

The angel continues to visit the island, from time to time, to guide the troop in our spiritual growth. As we matured in the Lord and our training was being passed down from generation to generation, the angel made fewer and fewer visits. But even in our time, he occasionally comes with a message or encouraging word. As a result of his leadership and the grace and mercy of God, this has been a Christian Island Nation for over 250 years.

As great as that all sounds, and it is something to be proud of, our Christian Nation is a fragile state of being. Our Christian status only stands from one generation to the next. It's up to each generation to pass on the teachings of Jesus to the next generation. If there is one breakdown between generations; if the message is not passed on to the younger generation a collapse in our Christianity occurs. With no one to teach the next generation, then, we might revert back to our old ways. In our case, that could mean a warring nation not founded in Christ. He is faithful to us and will never leave us; therefore, we must be faithful to Him and obey His commandments and stipulations."

Now Maw leaned forward, looking into the eyes of each one there with her own deep brown eyes. She stared with those eyes that were filled with knowledge and experience from her many years on earth.

Then in a low non-intimidating, but caring voice Maw said, "I want to bring this message down to a personal level to each one of you. The continuation of this Christian Nation and peaceful island life depends on you; it is your responsibility, and cannot be ignored or passed on to someone else. It is up to you to learn the Word of God, write it in your hearts; and when it is time, pass on that knowledge to your own offspring. Their eternal life depends upon that knowledge. I must also add a warning; you must understand that just being on this island, being a member of this troop, or having Christian parents *cannot* make you a Christian. Those things cannot make you a Christian any more than hanging from a coconut tree with the coconuts will make you a coconut.

What makes you a Christian comes from within your own heart and your own commitment to Christ. Becoming a Christian is a personal decision that each individual must make on his or her own. It is the decision to accept or reject Christ as their personal Savior; anyone who does not accept Jesus, automatically rejects Him. Once we accept Jesus, we follow Him, we want to learn more about Him; and we have a desire to tell everyone we can about how Jesus saved us.

Now, my love ones, you know the history of Monkey Island, you know what our ancestors had to endure so that we may live here in peace and freedom. You know about the angel who has guided us through our trials and taught us the ways of God. And you know about Christianity and how we became rooted in the love of our Savior Jesus Christ. You have, also, learned about your own responsibility to yourself, your family, the troop, and the future of the troop. Those are a lot of responsibilities; but feel confident in the Lord who has given you the ability to handle it all. If you didn't have the capability, He would not have given you the responsibility."

When Maw stopped speaking, everyone just sat in silence, each to his own thoughts, all knowing that they were in a special place. They were part of a group that had been "set aside" by God, and on ground that had been touched by Him; and all had a responsibility to maintain that relationship with their Savior. Knowledge could be passed on by others, but their individual responsibility was theirs alone. And he or she, alone, will be held accountable to God for the decisions they make and actions that they take, or do not take.

As the audience began to stir, Maw said, "If any of you have questions or just want to talk more about what you have heard get with your parents, one of the troop elders, the pastor or me."

She, then, singled out Stan, saying, "Go back to your camp and think through all the material you have heard over the past few days; then, in a few days return for another visit with me."

CHAPTER TEN

STAN MUST FACE REALITY

After four days of walking the beach alone, while running all these new concepts through his mind; Stan still could not make heads or tails out of any of all the information Maw had presented over those two days, at the cave.

He thought, "From the very beginning of landing on this island, everything is the completed opposite of what I had ever seen, heard, read or been taught."

He said to the sands beneath his feet, "Here I am, stuck on this island with hardly anything to help me survive. And even if I do live, what do I live for? I don't know if my friends made it to safety. My wife and kids will most likely never know what became of me. I will never be able to show them how much I truly love them. All of this is weighting on my mind, and I can't even get past the 'talking monkeys'. I really don't know if they are really talking; or, am I just going crazy?" Stan was feeling sorry for himself, and was beginning to be depressed.

Maw anticipated that this, overload of, information may have a negative impact on their island guest; so, for Stan's safety, she had him secretly watched to ensure no harm came to him. Maw had been receiving regular reports about Stan; but by the fifth day, he still had not returned to meet with her. Maw was beginning to seriously worry about Stan. She knew that it was not good for him to be alone all this time; so, she sent Tree Top to fetch Stan, and bring him back to camp.

Tree Top found Stan sitting on some rocks at the water's edge staring out to sea. "Hi pal, what's up?"

Stan did not hear him because he was deep within his own thoughts and self-pity.

Tree Top again, greeted Stan as he got closer to the rocks were Stan was positioned, "Stan's what's going on, we haven't heard from you?"

Stan was, at first, startled by the intruder; but he quickly recovered, "Oh, hi, Tree Top. I was just sitting here going over all my options."

"Great, run them by me," said Tree Top.

Without even thinking, Stan just blurted out, "That's my problem; I don't have any options. It's me on this island with nowhere to go or any way to get there. There is no one to care about what happens to me, and I'm totally cut off from all those I love back home."

"Now Stan," Tree top broke in, "We care about you. That is why Maw sent me over here to check up on you; and, to get you to come back with me to talk with her. And it's not only us, Stan; it's obvious to all of us that God greatly cares for you. Why else would He have sent His angel to pull you from the sea and deliver you to our shores? Stan, my friend, you need to count your blessings and thank God for what he has done and is doing for you. If it was not for God, you would have been lost at sea and have been fish bait weeks ago. So Stan, why not walk back to the troop with me."

Stan agreed half heartedly, "Why not, it's not like I have anything else to do."

"Keep your chin up, Stan. I know you don't see any hope yet, but don't give up now."

They walked together as Tree Top tried to make "small talk" to keep Stan's mind off his troubles. When Stan and Tree Top arrived in the camp, they were met by Maw who gave Stan a big hug. A number of other monkeys also came up to greet Stan letting him know they also cared.

Maw said, "I'm glad to see you. We all have been worried sick about you. It's not often that we get a guest on the island. We just want to make sure you are okay and getting along as best you can under the circumstances. How have you been doing these last few days? Come sit with me in the shade, and let's talk."

Stan did not want to expose his feeling; but, he couldn't help himself when all his emotions just poured out like a bucket of dirty water being dumped on pure white sand.

"Maw, I am doomed! There is no hope for me! I'll never see my wife again; I'll never see my children again, or any of my family. I let down my three friends who were on my boat; I'm sure they all drowned. I don't know why God didn't just let me drown with them. I did so much wrong in my past, and I have no way of making things right or even saying I'm sorry."

Stan took a deep breath of air and started right back. "I listened to the terrible things that happened to your ancestors, and I empathize with you. I really do; but, at least, you all had others to start over with; I have nothing or no one. When you told me there were six other men, before me, on the island; I had a ray of hope. But, anything I had to cling to was lost when you said, 'None of them made it off the island alive.' I'm sorry Maw. You all have been so kind to me; I am very grateful for what the troop has done for me. I would not have even made it off the beach, that first day, if it were not for Skippy. But now, I have come to the conclusion that I'm shipwrecked and stranded with no way out."

With that said, he hung his head and stared at the ground, waiting to hear a response from Maw. He was fully expecting Maw to try to cheer him up.

Maw put her hands on Stan's shoulders and held him at arm's length saying, "It is true that a chain of events starting with a storm and that shipwreck brought you to our shores. But son, listen to me; the real 'shipwreck' has not even occurred yet. The real wreck will come from within, when God brings you to your knees. Then, you will see yourself for what you are and Him for what He is: your smallness and His greatness. Once you have been stripped of all your false pride, stand 'naked' wrapped in your own sin and shame, and stop trying to get yourself out of life's mess; you will understand that only through Him you can be saved. Stop trying to work things out on your own terms; repent, and turn wholeheartedly to God. You will be broken all the way down, and then God will build you up. He will rebuild you in a way that can be used for His glory. Stan, it has been revealed to me that one day you will leave this island; but that day will not come until your mind, heart, and soul all line up with the 'Will of God'.

Stan, you have more going for you than you realize: you have your life that was almost lost, clean water to drink, you are eating regularly, you also have shelter to protect you from the elements, and us to keep you company. Granted, this may not be the level of comfort you are accustom to, but God provided what you needed, not what you may have wanted. And even though you rebelled against God and ran away from Him; He did not leave or abandon you. One more thing, you, more than anyone, should know how much He loves you. He sent an angel from heaven to pick you up and carry you out of what was sure to be a watery grave. Now you need to stop telling God how big your troubles are; and tell your troubles how big your God is."

Stan stood there wide eyed, as each word that Maw spoke hit him like right hooks and left jabs coming from a world class boxer; each solidly striking its mark. There was no getting away from the hard "punches" that Maw was putting down.

"Maw do you think this is God's way of punishing me?" Stan asked.

She replied, "I don't know God's mind; but He didn't put you on that boat to go on an extended party with your buddies. He didn't tell you not to pay attention to the changing weather conditions. And He didn't tell you to drink all that alcohol, which, in turn, impaired your judgment to make good decisions at sea. No, Stan, you did those things to yourself. Sometimes we make poor choices in life, and then have to face the consequences for our mistakes. I once heard someone wise say, 'You can't dance with the devil, then ask why you are still in hell.' But this is what I do know; God is not yet finished with you. He has a plan for your life, and He is giving you another opportunity to fulfill that which you were called to do."

CHAPTER ELEVEN

HEAVEN OPENS

A gain Stan walked home late that evening, but this time was different. He did not feel as alone as he did on other occasions.

He wondered, "Could this 'monkey' be right? How could she be so wise and know so much about so many things?"

Then he remembered something from his childhood Bible Study days, 'God works in mysterious ways.' "Of course He does, He is God, He can do anything He wants. If He wants to make animals that can talk and reason, why shouldn't He?"

Stan also recalled the story from the Bible where God used a donkey to talk to its rider. The donkey had more sense than the human in that story. "Donkey – monkey, what's the difference? God can use anything or anybody to get His message across."

For the first time since coming to the island, Stan saw Maw and the other monkeys, not as monkeys, but as God's creations with special gifts given to them by Him. Stan didn't realize it at the time; but, he was already starting to shed that pride that Maw was talking about.

That night the words that Maw spoke kept playing over and over in Stan's head. Then suddenly, a wave of emotions came out of his mind and into his heart. His past was right there in front of him, and a lot of what he saw was ugly. There was no getting around it, or trying to forget it. He knew that he had to deal with his past, now; or it would be on him like a wet blanket for the rest of his life. On one hand, something was telling him that "we" will get though this; we always have worked our way out trouble. But Stan's heart was telling him to turn all his problems over to Jesus Christ, who has already paid the price for his sin on the cross at Calvary.

Stan rolled out of his make-shift bed into the sand and cried like a baby. This time, the tears were not for himself, but for the way he had forsaken God. Right there in the sand, under the bright Caribbean night sky, Stan repented for each and every sin he could remember; he asked God to forgive him. The heavy cloud of sin and shame was lifted from his shoulders that very night. For the remainder of the night he slept calmly, like never before.

11.1 You Can't Contain It

The next day, Stan awoke late in the morning, after having his first good night's rest on the island. For the first time, he saw the real beauty of the land and surrounding sea. He thanked God that he was right here, in this moment. He jumped up and ran toward the monkey cave. He couldn't wait to tell Maw and his "friends" what had happened during the night.

Upon arrival, Stan burst into the cave clearing on a full run, out of breath, and frightening many that saw this "wild man" break the tranquility of their home. He was yelling, "Where is Maw? "Where is Maw? I must see Maw!"

The big guy, Max, was the first to reach Stan. Max grabbed him and asked, "What is wrong, what has happened to you?"

Stan was very animated and was not making much sense, "I'm good, I'm good! Where is Maw?"

Max said, "Slow down, and calm down then I'll send for Maw."

By this time, a crowd had gathered around Max and Stan. Everyone was trying to hear what was taking place. They had all known Stan, now, for over a month; and they had never seen him act this way. Maw, too, had seen all the commotion and worked her way through the crowd to where Max was holding onto Stan.

Maw told Max to, "Let Stan go."

Max released his grip on Stan; then, Stan embraced Maw, but was talking so fast she could not understand him. All she could make out was "God..., angel..., saved..., and sleep".

Maw ordered Stan, "Stop talking, take a deep breath and start over, slowly this time."

Wiping away tears from his eyes, Stan apologized; and then told Maw, and all who where there, what had happen the previous night in his camp. When Stan had finished, he stood exhausted; but grinning from ear to ear. It felt good to acknowledge the Lord, honor Him, and give praise to Him.

Max broke the silence, "This calls for a celebration."

Maw added, "It's a time for thanksgiving. One of God's lost sheep has returned to the flock."

Within minutes, the drums were tapping out a beat; monkeys were singing and dancing. They went from zero to full blown party time in "2.4 seconds".

Stan smiled to himself, "Look at big Max go; he is a real party animal- no pun intended. It's true these guys are a lot of fun. As my people friends would say, they are as fun as a 'barrel of monkeys'. I am blessed to have such good friends."

As the celebration went on, everyone was telling Stan how happy they were for him. They were glad to welcome him into the brotherhood of Christ. At one point during the dancing, little Debra jumped from the ground up into Stan's arms; so, that she could dance with him. Everyone had a good time, especially Stan.

11.2 Spiritual Growth

At the end of this impromptu celebration and before Stan departed for his camp, Maw invited him to stay. "Stan I would like you to move in with us. I worry that you get too lonely down there on the beach by yourself. You should be here, with friends, those who care for you." Debra and some of the other infants, who were listening, started pleading with him to stay.

Stan respectfully declined the offer, "I promise that I will be okay. I feel like I need this time to think and pray, alone. However, I will come back for a visit every day."

Maw said, "That's fine Stan, but our offer stands open. You are welcome to come live with us, if ever you change your mind."

Stan appreciated the gracious offer, "Thank you all so much." Then he headed for his beach camp.

Stan did go by the monkey cave every day, as he said he would. He talked with his friends, worshipped with them, and ate with the troop. And he worked the plantation, alongside those who were so willing to help him, in his time of need.

One day as he was tilling the field, he thought, "How ironic is this, the ancestors of these monkeys were dragged from their homes against their will to work someone else's plantation. And, now, generations later, these guys are working their own land. As the Bible says, God will take what others meant for evil and turn it to good for those who love Him.

In one of the many talks that Maw and Stan continued to have, she told him their "secret" to having a happy life. "The key to real long lasting happiness is found through God. You can surround yourself with all the things that the world has to offer, but if you are not right with God, all you have is for nothing. The physical self cannot be complete without the spiritual self lining up with the 'Will of God'."

"Here on the island God has given us all we have, and all we need to support the troop and our families:

> We have a never-ending supply of food from the sea.
>
> We have an abundance of food on land, as long as we manage it well and don't abuse the earth.
>
> We have several fresh water sources that, thank God, never run dry.
>
> We have a strong natural shelter, in the cave, that keeps us dry in the rain and safe during storms.
>
> God has equipped us with clothing that never wears out.
>
> He has blessed us with beautiful weather.
>
> We have no enemies, thanks to our Savior.
>
> And, we are surrounded by family and friends who all love each other.

We don't want or need anything else. What more could we want or need? And if you know of something, I don't want to hear about it. It was not meant for us, or God would have provided it. We are content with what we have; life is good here just the way God made it."

Maw continued, "That's what I call physical life. It's beautiful here; but when we die we can't take anything from this world with us. That's what makes the spiritual life so much more important. Spiritual happiness comes through contentment with God, who is more valuable than anything that can be found in this world. Jesus Christ and the Holy Spirit are the keys to life everlasting, because our own spirit will live on forever. Our inner happiness comes by knowing God through His Son, and living our lives here on earth accordingly."

Maw looked into Stan's eyes, "Do you understand all that I am telling you?"

Stan nodded his head, indicating that he did; and then Maw went on with her teaching.

"Once our basic needs are met, happiness becomes a state of mind. The joy and peace that the Lord puts in our hearts begins to flow out like a river of life to those around us. Anyone who, in turn, sees what we have through this out pouring of love, will want that same thing we have in their own lives. When we have God in us, He is just too big to contain; His love must flow out of us into the world. This is God's plan for growing the Kingdom and saving the lost. Our part is not to stifle the out pouring of Christ; we are to let it shine for all to see.

With this joy and peace within you, that only the Lord can give, you can be happy anywhere you find yourself. You can be content no matter what happens. You can come to a secluded island while on your way to have a good time somewhere else; or you can be taken from your own home and forced aboard a 'slave ship' before arriving here. Whatever the case may be, when we have the Lord on our side, we will be safe. When this life ends, we have a better life waiting for us in heaven."

Stan's soul was full; and it was now supper time; so, he and Maw went to have their physical bodies replenished.

11.3 Life On The Island Continues

Maw would continue to tutor Stan and be his spiritual guide. She coached him, recited scripture. Often, the two of them would go into the cave where the Bible was kept to read together.

At one point, Stan commented, "I can hardly believe the condition of this book with it being so old and used so much." Maw looked at him in disbelief. "Stan you have been with us all these months, surely your faith is stronger than that. Remember all the things that has happened on this island with you, and all that occurred here way before your arrival. This Bible came from God. If He can make the world and the universe and have them last as long as He wants; don't you think He can make a Bible last for those who love Him and want to know more about Him."

Stan was embarrassed by what he said. "Maw, you are so right! I blurted that out without thinking it through. I still have a tendency to see things through my worldly eyes, and speak before I filter the information through my heart."

"I understand Stan; we all do that from time to time." Maw continued, "We are all growing constantly in the Lord, and we never reach a point in this life where we know everything and are perfect. Only God is perfect! We just keep pressing on. The important thing to remember is when you stumble or fall; you get right back up, ask for forgiveness and carry on in the way Jesus would have you live."

Stan thought, "If only I grow to be as wise as this monkey."
Stan was learning and maturing as a Christian at a good pace. Of course, there were no outside distractions here on the island, which provided an excellent culture for learning. And Stan spent a lot of time with Maw "in search of God".

Maw often said, "If you seek the Lord, you will find Him. God comes to those who love Him and want Him in their lives."

Maw had been talking with the pastor about Stan and saying he has been such a good student of the Word.

The pastor asked, "Do you think he is ready to speak before the whole congregation at one of our Sunday meetings?"

Maw replied, "Pastor, I do believe he is ready. Stan telling his story would be good for him and uplifting to the church."

The pastor agreed to talk with Stan about giving his testimony in a future service.

The pastor did follow-up with Stan, who reluctantly agreed to the proposal. His apprehension came from fear of rejection and what others might say. On the other hand, he knew that he had to give praise to his Lord.

In a prayer Stan said, "Yes Lord, I will be obedient to You. This is the least thing I can do for You. It will be an honor to tell others what You have done for me."

Several weeks later, Stan was ready. The pastor had announced the week before that Stan would be speaking in Church that following week; so, everyone was excited and looking forward to this Sunday. When the time came, the group was deadly quite; you could have heard one of those tropical bugs crawling on the cave wall. Through a flood of tears and emotions, Stan told his life story, and how he had been saved. He told about all the great opportunities in Christ he had, but neglected, he instead, rebelled and ran from God. He told all the good and the bad, not leaving much out of the details.

Stan said, "At one time in my life, I thought I was 'on top of the world' doing it my way. I thought I had everything under control; but then I found myself almost losing my life at the bottom of the sea."

Stan's testimony was spellbinding to the monkeys who had not been exposed to the world beyond their shores. They were blessed hearing about Stan's transformation, but also had many questions about the world he had come from.

After church, some of the adults asked him about how monkey's live in "his world"; and what is the world like beyond Monkey Island, Stan hated to answer the question, but he was not going to lie either.

"Well, there are only a few places in the United States where monkeys roam free; in fact, the only place that I have seen is in Florida around a place called Silver Springs. I'm sorry to tell you this, but most monkeys in America live in zoos and are on exhibit for people to come by and view them. They are well taken care of, but are forced to live in cages or some type of enclosure made to resemble their natural habitat. Believe me, when I tell you that you are so blessed to be living here, free, surrounded by your loved ones, and free from interference by outsiders".

11.4 Young Men Will See Visions & Old Men Dream Dreams (Acts 2:17 NLT)

Life went on as usual on the island where Stan has now lived for nearly a year among the monkeys. Then, one night, Stan was visited by an angel in his dreams. The angel told him that it was time for him to prepare to leave the island. The angel told him how to construct a raft and make a sail to push the vessel through the waters. He had a vision of the completed raft.

The angel said to Stan not to worry, "The Lord will be with you on this journey."

Stan awoke and immediately went to share the news, "Maw, you will not guess what happened?"

"Good morning Stan. Well, then, don't make me guess. What is it? And tell it to me slowly? You know you have a tendency to talk fast when you get excited."

Stan told Maw all about the dream, his vision, and what the angel had said. He told her every detail down to exactly how the raft and sail was to be built, what was to be taken onboard with him, what part of the island to leave from and what time of day to sail off.

Upon ending his story, Maw was asked, "What do you think?"

"I certainly believe you were visited by an angel; and I told you months ago that one day you would leave this island. The Lord had revealed that to me. Since you have been here, you have both sought and found God. He has forgiven you and has given you a new spirit and heart after His own. If you remember, I told you that these things would happen before you could move on beyond these shores. And now, it seems that you have pleased God. He has prepared you for what is to come. He is ready to send you on your next step, in life, to fulfill the mission He has called you to do. You will be missed here, but you now have more important work to do. Never forget that it was God who saved you form the sea and your own sin; and it is He who is giving you this fresh start."

CHAPTER TWELVE

A VISION TURNS TO REALITY

Maw made a commitment to Stan, "We will help you build the raft and make preparations for your voyage."

Hearing those words made Stan both happy and afraid at the same time. It meant that his vision was about to move into reality.

Maw, being very intuitive, said, "Be brave my son, it is God who sent this message to you. You are to follow His directions and have faith that He will deliver on His word. God will never start you on a mission, and then not provide all that you need to finish the job. Just trust in Jesus!"

Stan, filled with mixed emotions, could not say a thing; he hugged Maw. As excited as he was about going home, the thought of leaving the safety of the island on a handmade raft scared him. Island life is all that he has come to know over the past year.

Stan thought, "The angel's visit brought back memories of the shipwreck and my days of being tossed around in the sea like a fishing cork; all of which, until now, seemed so long ago. And, how will my own family react to me showing up, 'out of the blue'? Have they given up on me, by now, and moved on with their own lives? Who could blame them?"

The only thing Stan could do was trust God. This thought flashed in his mind, "There is no turning back."

Maw broke the awkward silence, "Tell me what you need to get the raft started. I'll talk with Max and have him get some of the big guys from the troop together to start gathering the materials in the morning."

As slow and laid back as island life is, when plans are made the monkeys immediately "jump into action". There is no need to spend a lot of time determining a complicated plan of attack.

Stan laid out the design as told by the angel, "The raft is to be 18' long by 10' wide. We will need a total of eight trees with a twelve inch diameter to make up the two pontoons. And we will need smaller diameter trees ten foot in length for the deck. In addition, we will need other logs to lash onto the pontoons at the bow and stern to hold everything together. We'll need many long strips of inner tree bark to tie all the logs together. We, will, also, need five additional logs to use as rollers to get the raft off the beach and into the water. Once the raft is constructed, we will make the cabin, sail, mast and rudder."

"Maw, I never thought of this; but how will we cut down the trees that we will need for the raft?"

Maw took Stan into the cave where they keep all the tools that were salvaged from "their ship" long, long ago.

There she pointed out several axes and said, "You can use one of these. No one has used these axes, since our ancestors first used them to clear a section of the jungle for our plantation. They are old, but they still work, especially with a big strong man like you behind one."

The next morning, a group of males were waiting for Stan when he arrived at the camp. They headed out into the jungle right-a-way; and, in short time, located the trees that would be cut into logs needed for the pontoons. They cut down the trees and carried each one to the beach. They, then, rolled the logs into the water and floated them down to the point where the angel said to launch the raft. The raft would be assembled there. After all the logs were staged on the sand, Stan thanked his friends.

He said, "Guys, that is enough work for one day. Let's go home, get something to eat and rest."

To save time during the raft construction, Stan took advantage of Maw's offer to move in with the troop.

The second day was used to form the two pontoons. The pontoon logs were laid out in two sets of four logs each. The two eighteen-foot logs were placed in the center, allowing a two-foot gap between them; these logs were assembled on top the "roller logs". On the outboard side of the first logs the seventeen-foot logs were laid, then the sixteen-foot logs were laid down, and last the fifteen-foot logs were put into place. Each side, consisting of four logs, was the same; when put together the logs formed a wedge at the bow of the raft. All four logs of each pontoon were securely tied together at one foot intervals.

Days three and four were used to gather the deck logs and other logs needed for the raft. As the guys were hauling the logs to the build site; others were tying them across the two pontoons. The deck logs would be used to hold the whole structure together. The troop females were interested in the details of the build and wanted to help with construction.

Stan stood, with his arms stretched wide, facing the construction site and said to the work crew, "This has turned out to be a real community project. I could not be more blessed."

Prepared to leave the safety of the island.

When Monday morning came, the crew started work on the raft's cabin, which would be eight-foot wide, five-foot deep and four-foot high, upon completion. It will be closed at the front and on the sides and open in the rear. They placed the cabin on the forward section of the raft deck, leaving a one-foot walkway on each side and a five foot open deck at the rear. The crew covered the cabin with a thatched roof that would keep out sun and rain. A twelve-foot mast was mounted to and centered on the inner front wall of the cabin; here they hang the sail.

Meanwhile, some of the females who were not working on the main construction project were busy building the, six-foot by eight-foot, sail frame made of two-inch diameter hardwood poles, and smaller vertical supports, placed every foot apart. The crew, then, attached braded inner bark strips, horizontally, to the frame every four inches. Next they wove banana leaves between the bark strips, over lapping them to make a solid sail.

The remaining task was to make the rudder, which was crafted from a single twelve foot log and secured at the center of the raft on the aft deck.

Every detail of the raft was exactly as the angel had instructed.

CHAPTER THIRTEEN

STAN SAYS FAIRWELL

As construction on the raft was nearing completion, Maw called Stan to the side for what would be their final private meeting together.

Maw started the conversation, "Stan, I congratulate you on the progress you have made in your spiritual growth, since coming to the island. I am blessed to have helped you on your journey back to God and by the personal relationship that we have forged together."

But then, the tone of the conversation took a solemn turn. Maw continued in a more serious manor, "From the minute you arrived on the sands of this island, your safety was in our hands. When you were laid on the sand, Skippy brought you coconuts; so, that you could survive that first day. Then, we welcomed you and took you into our confidence. We shared our food with you, opened our home to you, and offered our friendship. We helped nurture you back to full strength, and guide you back to Christ. I believe you have come to see that this island is a special place, which is blessed by God. I tell you these things, because when you leave here you owe us your loyalty. By that, I mean, when you go back into your world, you must protect our safety and security.

You cannot tell anyone about this troop, our interactions with you, or even the location of this island. To do so would mean the destruction of our very way of life and the island as we know it. Our recovery from the disaster that God saved us from, 250 years ago, would be in jeopardy with even a leak of our existence. So, as much as you have depended on us for your survival; we must now depend on you for ours."

Stan said, "I fully understand and agree to your demand. I swear an oath to never reveal the location of the island or discuss the troop. 'What happened on Monkey Island will stay on Monkey Island!' Your secrets are safe with me."

Stan and Maw then, tearfully held each other before breaking out from their private meeting.

With the construction job completed, a celebration and goodbye party was planned for the next day. It would be a full blown "party like a monkey" time. It was very much like the welcoming party they had given Stan a year earlier. Once again, the drums were tapping out a joyful tune; everyone was dancing, and there was all the food to go with a fine ho-down. These monkeys knew how to put on a party! The big difference, this time, was that Max was not providing security; he, too, was right up in all the fun. However, within all the festivities, there was an underlying sadness about the upcoming island departure; but the full impact of those feeling would not be evident until tomorrow.

Later that evening, following the party, the raft was loaded with provisions exactly as the angel had instructed. Other than Stan providing direction, as relayed to him by the angel, not much else was said; everyone worked with a heavy heart. The raft was loaded with thirty coconuts; ten were left whole and twenty were filled with fresh water and the hole sealed with a tightly rolled leaf. Supplies, also, included a rock to crack open the coconuts to be eaten, thirty bananas, sixty oysters and Stan's two fishing poles. When the task was completed, everyone quietly walked back to the cave for the night.

As the troop slept, Stan laid on his mat thinking and praying. He was restless and, at one point, got up and went on a moonlight walk along the beach. Unintentionally, he ended up at the raft, where he sat on one of the pontoons and thought about what was going to happen at sunrise. There was no denying it; he was scared of the unknown.

"How time changes things," Stan thought, "a year ago, I hated the fact of landing of this tropical island with no one to talk to and no apparent way off. And now, a year later, I have many friends, a raft provided by God, and I'm reluctant to leave the same island that I didn't want to be on in the first place."

And then, he thought about his wife and children. What will they think about his sudden return? "Surely, by now, they must think I have died at sea. I wonder if they have moved on with their own lives and forgotten all about me. I wonder if my wife is seeing anyone new; how could I blame her? I'm sure my kids will be glad to see me; no one can replace their birth father. Will they be happy or angry after not hearing from me for over a year? Financially, the family should have been okay; they had our savings and my retirement to live on. I wonder if I am classified as missing, or am I 'officially deceased'? I hope not. I have all these questions and concerns; but I'm sure everyone is going to have a lot more questions for me after they get over the impact of me being alive."

Maw had seen Stan leave the cave during the night, but decided it would be best to leave him to his own thoughts. She, too, had a restless night worrying about Stan and him sailing off into the unknown in a few hours. Now, the "big day" was upon them. Maw got everyone up and they all walked to the launch site. There they found Stan asleep on the raft.

CHAPTER FOURTEEN

BON VOYAGE

The noise of the troop approaching the raft awoke Stan. He was disorientated, at first, but quickly pulled himself together.

He jumped to his feet, "Hi guys. I must have fallen to sleep. Thanks for coming to see me off."

The pastor spoke up, "First, my friend, you are not going anywhere unless we all pitch in to get this heavy raft into the water. But before we do that, we all want to say good-bye, give you our best wishes, and pray with you before you sail off. And if you don't mind, I would like to bless this craft in the name of our Lord. I know the raft came from Him, but all the same, we want to pray over you and this vessel."

The pastor led the group in a prayer. "Lord, we ask You to please keep Your hand on this raft making it sea worthy. Cover Stan with Your 'wings' of protection making his voyage safe, and a speedy trip home to his love ones. We, also ask, that Stan always remember You. May Your glory is seen in him all the remaining days of his life; and may those days be long and happy. We pray in the name of Jesus, Amen."

Every single monkey from the troop took his/her turn to step up on the raft to personally give their departing wishes. There were many tears that fell on the deck that morning; but perhaps Debra took this last meeting the hardest. She had grown quite fond of Stan, and she was no longer the little infant that sat in Stan's lap at "story time". She was now almost full grown and had spent a lot of time with Stan over the past year. The last of all to approach Stan was Maw. She embraced him, but there was not much left to say between the two. It had all been said before. This was the teacher and student saying good-bye to one another; it was two old friends who had grown fond of each other and were now parting ways. Each knew that this would be the last time that they would ever see each other again. Spiritually, Maw knew Stan would be alright. Through the tears that Stan shed, she could feel the deep gratitude and love that Stan had for her.

But being the spiritual guide to Stan, she could not let him get off the island without one last bit of wisdom and a warning. "Stan, you came to us as a spiritual wreck and, now, you have found your way back to God. Listen to me closely. It's easy to be a Christian here; you are surrounded by other Christians who all want the same things as you: more of God. On the island, there are no outside distractions or others trying to lead you away from the Savior. But dear friend, where you are going there will be plenty of distractions and temptations. There will be those who will want to drag you back down into a world of sin, and there will be old 'friends' that will remind you of all the things you did before you turned to the Lord. You remain steadfast in the faith and pray to the Holy Spirit to give you strength to withstand all the attacks of the devil. And find yourself a good, strong Christian support system and church. You will be fine! We love you."

With all the farewells said, the troop and Stan "rolled" the raft into the water. Once in the water, Stan jumped onboard; while the adult monkeys continued to push the raft out to sea, past the small waves on this side of the island. Once there, Stan lifted the sail, and the monkeys returned to their island. When the sail was set, Stan turned to see all the monkeys still standing on the beach waving to him. He waved back, remembering the first time he waved back to the young monkey that was with Tree Top on the beach. That first time he had waved to the monkey, he felt foolish, as a grown man, waving to a monkey. Now, his heart was filled with love and admiration for these same monkeys, his dear friends. That first encounter with "talking monkeys" seemed so long ago; however, his time on the island already felt like light years apart from this present moment.

Stan thought, "So much has happened in a year; and I learned so much from this unbelievable source of information and wisdom: monkeys." Aloud, he said, God, thank You for Your love and forgiveness; and thank You for these monkeys You sent into my life."

The troop remained on the sand beach until the "hairless white monkey" was out of site; then, one by one, they started drifting back to "island life as usual". Maw was the last to leave the beach, that morning, as she stood deep in thought and prayer. Her "son" was gone, but never will be forgotten. He will, now, be forever part of "Monkey Island History". After Stan was out of sight and long gone, she, too, then slowly walked back to the cave.

CHAPTER FIFTEEN

AT SEA

After only thirty minutes out to sea, Stan turned to look at the island one more time, but it could not be seen. It was as if Monkey Island had just vanished or had been swallowed by the sea. Stan was standing all alone on the raft deck, but he was not feeling lonely because of the One who was living inside of him. With the sail doing its job, Stan stood with his back to the breeze looking out over the top of his sleeping quarters at the big "empty" sea.

He thought, "What a sight I must look like with hair past my shoulders and an unkempt beard to my chest; still wearing the same shorts, shoes and shirt I came to the island with".

The shirt and shoes did not see much wear during the time spent on the island, but the shorts had seen better days.

"Oh well, this is a fashion statement from where I came from. It's the latest in 'island wear'; 'all the men' are wearing it this season."

With that he had to laugh at himself; and then he wondered, "How long will it take him to reach land or be rescued by a passing ship?"

After three and a half days at sea and not having much rest, Stan was exhausted. The sun was high and hot at mid day, when he crawled inside the shelter for a nap. He fell fast into a deep; deep sleep, that lasted well into the following day. When he woke, he had no idea what day it was or how long he had been sleeping. Then, he remembered that a sound of some sort had awakened him. He was still lying there trying to place the sound, when he heard it again.

"That is a horn, *that is a ship's horn!*" Stan yelled out.

He jumped from his mat and could not believe his eyes. His raft was on a collision course with a huge cruise ship headed north. He dropped the sail and started jumping up and down, franticly, flagging the ship with both arms. He did not stop until he heard three short blasts from the ship's horn signaling that they had spotted him, and the ship reduced its speed.

The Rescue!

A few minutes later a small landing craft was lowered into the water and was speeding in his direction.

"Praise God, I'm being rescued just as the angel had promised."

As he was stepping off the raft onto the landing craft he noticed that the logs were starting to come apart; only minutes earlier the vessel was strong and sea worthy. By the time they reached the cruise ship, the once sturdy raft was lying flat in the ocean completely broken apart.

One of the sailors said, "You are a lucky man. Another few minutes and you would not have had a raft at all."

Stan replied, "No my friend, that raft was given to me by God. And when God gives you something; He makes a promise that it will last until its purpose is completed. That raft was fine until I stepped off of it; then, it was not needed any longer."

Before he fully realized what happened, he was lifted onto the deck of the ship; and, then, rushed below by security personnel to the ship's medical facilities. He was examined by a doctor who determined that Stan was in good physical and mental health. He was, then, released to the First Officer who took a detailed report from Stan. Stan was able to produce his identification, which he still carried in his wallet.

Stan told the officer, "My boat sunk, over a year ago, while in route to the Bahamas on a fishing trip with three friends. As far as I know, I was the only survivor. After the boat sank, I spent several days in the rough seas before being washed onto the beach of a small tropical island. The island was unoccupied. I was able to survive with the emergency kit I had in my life vest and my faith in God, which greatly increased over my time on the island.

This is a story that would be repeated over and over during the upcoming days and weeks. Although the First Officer was skeptical of Stan's story; there was nothing to dispute Stan's account of the events. In their rush to get Stan off the raft and back to the ship, none of the sailors bothered to inspect the raft. Had they done so, someone may have questioned how the logs were cut with no available tools other than a pocket knife and hand saw from the survival kit in Stan's life vest. Stan chalked that one up to the Lord protecting the identity of Monkey Island. When asked how long he had been at sea on the raft, Stan was ambiguous for the same reason. He knew that based on ocean currents and wind speed, his distance could be calculated backwards from the point where he was found; so, he said he wasn't sure, but it was anywhere from fourteen to eighteen days. That way it would be impossible for anyone to find the correct location of the island where he had been marooned.

Stan was photographed and finger printed by Security. That, along with the ship's report, would be requested by US authorities, under these circumstances. He was then taken to the crew's quarters, where he was allowed to take his first hot shower in over a year. He stayed in the shower letting the soothing water wash all the dirt, grime, sea salt, emotions and fears down the drain. When he stepped out of the shower, he was handed two sets of new clothes and a pair of new shoes from the ship's stores. All his new gear were compliments of the ship's captain. Once dressed in one of his new outfits, he was fed and taken to the barber shop where he was given a shave and hair cut. Looking into the mirror, he saw the face of the "old Stan", but he smiled at the new person he had become on the inside.

Now washed, clean shaven, and wearing new clothes, he was escorted to the bridge to meet the Captain. The Captain had already read the reports and seen the "mug shots" of Stan before he arrived on the bridge.

"I trust that my crew has been taking good care of you. I have been informed of the extraordinary ordeal that you have been through. Ironically, our next port of call is Miami, Florida in two days. As I understand that is the port you last departed from a year ago."

Stan replied in the affirmative and the Captain continued, "As required, I have already reported this incident to the Port Authorities, Customs and the US Coast Guard; and I'm sure they will get Homeland Security and the FBI involved in verifying your identity. I hope you understand; these things are never just a simple matter.

But while we are at sea, you will be our quest. We have assigned you a cabin and a security team. You are 'requested' to dine in your quarters, and you will have limited movement while on the ship. You will not be allowed to talk with the other guests or crew members for safety reasons. A member of your security team will be with you, at all times, until you are turned over to US Authorities. Do you have any questions? I know you have gone through a lot; we will make your stay with us as pleasant as possible under these circumstances."

Stan did not have any questions for the Captain. He responded, "Captain, thank you and your crew for rescuing me and for being so kind to me while onboard your ship. I understand; every precaution needs to be taken for the safety for our country and our people."

The country's re-entry procedures caught him a little off guard; but, then, in this day of terrorism, security has to be a high priority. Stan understood that the Authorities had to be sure who he is, and that he was not off training with some radical group in another country for the past year. He was just glad to be going home and was willing to do whatever was necessary to get back to his family.

After a good night's sleep, in a real bed, Stan asked his guard, "Could we go up on the top deck to get some fresh air?"

His security guard agreed and cleared the request through the ship's bridge. It was still early when they walked out on deck where they found themselves all alone. The guard sat in a chair, against the bulkhead, where he could watch Stan and still give him a little freedom to walkabout. Stan observed a seagull perched on the handrail. He walked to the handrail and slowly inched his way toward the bird. When he was about five feet away from the bird, and out of earshot of his guard, Stan spoke to the seagull.

"I know you can talk; your secret is safe with me. You don't even have to answer me, but I have a favor to ask of you. For the past year, I have lived with the monkeys on Monkey Island. They helped me survive, all that time, and later helped me build a raft and sail away. I know that they are worried about me, and I don't have any way to get word back to them. If you go that way; would you be so kind as to let them know that I made it to safety?"

The bird did not speak, but he made eye contact with Stan and then flew away. Stan felt confident that his message would get through on the "animal pipeline".

CHAPTER SIXTEEN

HOME AT LAST

About an hour before the ship was scheduled to arrive in port, Stan was escorted back to his cabin and ordered to stay there until told otherwise. Security personnel remained posted outside his door. As soon as the ship docked, it was boarded by representatives from Homeland Security and the FBI, who escorted Stan off the ship into an interrogation room located in Custom's facilities. There, he was, again, fingerprinted with an electronic devise that used updated scanning technology and could instantly identify who he is. Then, more pictures of Stan were taken.

The Authorities verified Stan's identity through the fingerprint check. They had also checked into his background while he was in route back to the States. But knowing his identity and proving what he had been doing for the past year are two different things. He, again, had to repeat his story several times; while the investigators tried to pick out inconsistencies in his statement.

Stan thought, "If they don't believe this version of the story; they would never believe the whole truth. Instead of going home, they would be sending me to a mental health hospital to 'count pink elephants' in the room. But then, again, I have nothing to worry about; God will take care of me, whatever happens. I know God didn't bring me this far to have anything bad happen to me; His Will, will be done."

He didn't like not being totally truthful, but he took an oath to protect Monkey Island and the troop; God and the monkeys expected him to honor his oath.

Toward the end of the "interview" the investigator said, "Stan, in our review into the year-old sinking of your boat, we learned that the three men, also on that fishing trip, survived. Apparently they were picked up in a life raft by a fishing boat two days after the shipwreck."

Stan sighed in relief, broke down in tears then said, "Thank God for their rescue! Their welfare has been weighting heavy on my heart this past year."

In the meantime, Homeland Security contacted the local police department; and requested that their police chaplain go to Stan's residence to speak with his wife and family.

When the police chaplain arrived at Stan's house, he gently gave Stan's wife the news that her husband is alive and has been located. Once she got over the initial shock of this good news; arrangements were made for her and the children to be reunited with Stan. It would be a joyful time for the whole family.

Mean time, back on Monkey Island, the troop was celebrating the good news that they had received from a passing bird. They had been notified that "their son" had made it to safety and was being taken back to his home.

THE END

AUTHOR'S THOUGHTS

The Lord led me to write this book in a way that would be fun and exciting for my young readers and their parents. Stan's situation is typical of many of us in today's society. Hopefully, none of us will be lost at sea, when our "boat" is destroyed. But many of us find ourselves drifting endlessly in a lost world; and finding our hopes and dreams being smashed on the "rocks" of everyday life. There, we feel helpless and all alone, as if we are left stranded with no way out.

We can't always go back and fix all the things that we did wrong; we may not even be forgiven by the people we hurt. However, we can forgive those who hurt us, and we can, with the power of the Holy Spirit, move on and not make those same mistakes again. And like Stan, we can find salvation and redemption in our Lord Jesus Christ. Jesus is real, and he wants to be a part of your life. Seek the Lord with all your heart and you will find Him: Love.

READY FOR THE STORM

I see the storm clouds gathering in the distant sky.
At midday it begins to darken.
I hear the thunder clapping as the far off army prepares for war.
I see the faraway lightening as it flashes down at the earth.

As the storm builds I feel its approaching winds start to brush
against my face.
I know that the weak will be washed away by such a force that
will come.
The Lord told me that I would have to encounter many trials
in my life.
But He also told me that He would never leave or forsake me.

Oh Lord I walk in Your righteousness.
Daily I seek Your face and search Your word.
I pray to be in Your presence.
My God Your strength makes fear flee from me.

Now the sky is black within the storm,
The hard driving rain stings my face.
The thunder is as loud as cannons being fired from every
direction.
Lighting is striking at my feet and at my hand.

The faces of evil are all around.
The voice of defeat tells me to turn left or right.
Deceit rings in my ear,
He says do this or that and the storm will quite.

I reject those of the evil army.
I will not give in to the wicked,
His numbers are many and his lies are tempting.
But he is no match for the Almighty.

I draw my holy sword and stand to fight.
I may be struck; I may be knocked down,
But I will not be conquered.
Be it His will I will fight to the end.

I will fight because I am a child of God.
I will withstand because I am a solder in His army.
I have put on the Christian armor of the Lord.
In the end I will be more than a victor.

As I fight on I move through the storm.
I continually pray that the Lord maintains my strength.
The enemy starts to weaken,
I will not be defeated.

I look around and see that the Lord is my rear guard,
He is at my right hand and at my left.
God is at my front leading the fight.
No enemy can withstand His mite.

Now the clouds have cleared,
The battle has been won.
I am stronger now than before.
I with my Lord have conquered.

I stand humble but strong in the presence of my God.
He is my strength and He has taken me through the storm.
I stand with the conqueror's sword high above my head.
I scream "the victory belongs to God".

Robert W. Lailheugue
June 2014

OTHER BOOKS BY THIS AUTHOR

The Hunter and Little Joey
Christian Faith Publishing

If you liked "talking monkeys", you are going to love the "talking dogs" in this book. This is another Christian novel by Mr. Lailheugue that takes you on a journey of excitement, laughter and heartbreak. Little Joey is one, who like many of us, had to learn "the hard way". Intertwined into the plot are biblical lessons that the readers will be drawn to.

Coming soon:

Dog Behind the Badge
(Publisher TBD)

There is only one talking animal in this book. He is the canine partner of his police handler. This fiction novel is based on true stories that are told through the eyes and ears of the police dog. The story captures the adventures and the tight bond between the police handler and his close friend and canine partner; one where "Max" will save the life of his human partner. It is a bond that spills over into the family life as the police dog becomes a true member of his handler's family. The author and Max served as a canine team during the 1970's in Jefferson Parish, LA. This is another Christian novel you will not want to miss.

Seeking Da Lord
(Publisher TBD)

This is a Christian, children's picture book, written to include many of the Cajun French slang words and phrases that we often here in South Louisiana. It's a fun story that follows Boudreaux and Clotilde, around the United States, as they go in search of the Lord. Clotilde is willing to follow Boudreaux in his many escapades; but, she does pick up a "bit of an attitude" along the way. Come, travel with this couple as they ride the roads of America; taking us to many familiar landmarks in our great country.

ABOUT THE AUTHOR

Mr. Robert W. Lailheugue III is a veteran of the Vietnam War, having served in the U.S. Navy. Upon discharge from military service, he went to work for the largest sheriff's office in the State of Louisiana. As a police officer, Mr. Lailheugue worked in several different capacities including undercover vice squad officer, patrol officer, canine handler (both narcotics and patrol), bomb technician, sergeant (Patrol and Canine Divisions), and finally Commander of the Canine and Emergency Divisions. After leaving the sheriff's office, he went to work for a large nuclear utility company, where he started up and operated the security department at one of the company's nuclear power plants. He later moved out of security and moved into other management positions within the company before retiring in 2004.

He is married to his high school sweetheart and currently living in South Louisiana, where they have raised their two children. When not traveling, they attend the Harbor Church in Hammond, Louisiana, where they are actively serving in the Christian community. Mr. Lailheugue enjoys hunting, fishing and serving the Lord. He holds a bachelor's degree in criminal justice and has attended numerous law enforcement, security and management schools.